CLARA HUMBLE

and the
Kitten Caboodle

CLARA HUMBLE

and the
Kitten Caboodle

Anna Humphrey

Illustrations by Lisa Cinar

Owlkids Books

Owlkids Books acknowledges the financial support of the Canada Council for the Arts, the Ontario Arts Council, the Government of Canada through the Canada Book Fund (CBF), and the Government of Ontario through the Ontario Media Development Corporation's Book Initiative for our publishing activities.

Published in Canada by
Owlkids Books Inc.
10 Lower Spadina Avenue
Toronto, ON M5V 2Z2

Published in the United States by
Owlkids Books Inc.
1700 Fourth Street
Berkeley, CA 94710

Library and Archives Canada Cataloguing in Publication

Humphrey, Anna, 1979-, author
    Clara Humble and the kitten caboodle / Anna Humphrey ; illustrations by Lisa Cinar.

ISBN 978-1-77147-241-8 (hardcover)

    I. Cinar, Lisa, 1980-, illustrator II. Title.

PS8615.U457C529 2018   jC813'.6   C2017-907419-9

Library of Congress Control Number: 2017961187

Edited by Sarah Howden
Designed by Danielle Arbour and Alisa Baldwin

ONTARIO ARTS COUNCIL
CONSEIL DES ARTS DE L'ONTARIO
an Ontario government agency
un organisme du gouvernement de l'Ontario

Canada Council
for the Arts

Conseil des Arts
du Canada

Canadä

Manufactured in Altona, MB, Canada, in March 2018, by Friesens Corporation
Job #239822

A   B   C   D   E   F

 Publisher of Chirp, chickaDEE and OWL
www.owlkidsbooks.com

Owlkids Books is a division of  Bayard
CANADA

In memory of Siobhan Morgan Sheflin,
animal rescuer.
— A. H.

To my kittens, Andrea, Åsa, and Colleen.
— L. C.

Contents

The Birthday Chicken

Me and Bradley: We'd always been best friends.
We loved all the same things, from orange
Creamsicles to comic books (especially the non-
stop action-packed adventures of @Cat). And we
did everything together, from back-to-school shoe
shopping to swashbuckling. (It's a pirate thing.)

Our Halloween costumes last year.

Notice our
matching
sneakers and
peg legs?

But ever since that spring, when my best friend had appeared on *Smarty Pants*—a televised quiz show for fourth graders—he'd changed. Mostly, it was good. With his newfound confidence, Bradley had started raising his hand more in Ms. Smith's class. He'd even volunteered to be the emcee at the end-of-year school barbecue, announcing the winners of the egg-on-a-spoon race right into the microphone.

But things took a turn for the worse when we began building the Kitten Caboodle ... and, if I'm being honest, I should have seen it coming as far back as the day of Bradley's tenth birthday party: an afternoon that was supposed to be fun-filled but that ended up seriously sucking—literally—at least for me.

It was the second Sunday of July, and we were in Bradley's backyard, where the party was in full swing.

"Hiiiiii-yaaaah!" our friend Abby yelled. She was wearing a blindfold and waving a baseball bat around wildly. Even though she was only about four feet tall and had a teeny-tiny mouse-squeak of a voice, Abby had surprising strength and stamina. I didn't envy the pig-shaped piñata she was attacking.

On her third hit, the swine exploded, showering candy onto the grass. All the party guests rushed to pick some up—all the guests, that is, except for Bradley's new friend, Nelson.

"Nelson!" Bradley called. My best friend was kneeling on the lawn with two huge handfuls of packaged gumballs, Jolly Ranchers, and Fizz poppers. "Come get some."

Nelson just smiled and shrugged. "Thanks, but candy gets stuck in my braces." He went back to flipping through his magazine— or, actually, Bradley's magazine.

Nelson had given it to Bradley for his birthday, along with a

monthly subscription. It looked pretty boring—at least, compared with my gift (a genuine sno-cone machine that could do six different flavors), but Bradley had made a huge deal about how much he loved it, and I guess it was a thoughtful present. Plus, it went well with what Bradley's mom got him: his very own X-2000 metal detector, which according to Nelson was professional grade and super-lightweight, and even had an ultrasensitive DD coil—whatever that was.

Who was this Nelson kid anyway? you might be wondering. Bradley had met him just the week before at JTT Camp. (JTT's short for Junior Treasure Trackers.) And they got along so well that he'd scored a last-minute invite to the party.

In summers past, Bradley and I had always gone to the same camps, but that year, as school ended and it came time to choose, we just couldn't agree.

"JTT will be a different treasure-hunting adventure every day," Bradley had said, butt-bouncing on his couch with excitement. And it did sound fun—until you looked more closely.

"Local history lessons. Three-hour treasure treks. Geocaching excursions and a rust-removal workshop," I'd read off Bradley's mom's laptop. I couldn't help wrinkling my nose.

It wasn't that I didn't like treasure—Bradley and I had been digging holes in his yard for years, searching for buried artifacts. But there were just so many other cool camps to choose from.

In the end, I picked something else, but Bradley had his heart set on four weeks of JTT—the same four weeks, coincidentally, as his new friend, Nelson. It was good that they got along, because they were going to be removing a lot of rust together. And I was glad Bradley had a camp friend ... I just didn't understand why he'd picked Nelson. The guy was so serious.

"What about some SweeTarts, then?" Bradley suggested. "They're not sticky."

"No thanks." Nelson pushed his glasses up on his nose and flipped another page in the magazine.

"Just leave him alone," someone said. Even though I was busy picking Jolly Ranchers out of the grass and had my back turned—and regardless of the fact that he was mumbling through a mouthful of gumballs—I didn't have to guess who it was. "More candy for me that way," added Shane

When you're #1 at being the worst.

MOST LEAST FAVORITE PERSON OF THE YEAR

Biggs—my new neighbor and most least favorite person.

Just before Christmas, he and his mom bought my old neighbor Momo's house. Since moving in, not only had they ruined her prizewinning garden by never watering it and painted the whole place a sad color called "storm gray," they'd also cut down a big oak tree that used to be a home for squirrels and birds—just to make way for a basketball net Shane never used. And those weren't even the only reasons he was the worst.

Just two months before summer holidays, Shane had done his best to sabotage me and every other girl contestant who'd competed on the game show *Smarty Pants*. Then once school let out, my mother had insisted that I go be "neighborly." I'd knocked on Shane's door after dinner and invited him to do not one, not two, but three outstandingly fun things with me and Bradley—one of which involved applesauce, a catapult, and an inflatable clown. And every single time he'd said he was too busy, when it was obvious he was just sitting around playing Xbox.

Basically, Shane was mean and lazy, and unless there was something in it for him, he had no— and I mean ZERO—sense of adventure, and those are qualities I just cannot stand in a person.

"Don't you think you've got enough candy?" I said to Shane. His pockets were bulging, both his hands were full, and his mouth was too. "Jamila and Glenn hardly got any, and you're hogging it all."

"So?" he countered, smacking his gum. "They should have run faster when the piñata broke."

I put my hands on my hips and stared him down, but before I could let Shane know exactly what I thought of his bad attitude, Bradley cut in. "It's okay," he said. "I've got more candy inside. There's lots for everyone."

To my dismay, Bradley had decided to be friendly to Shane toward the end of the school year—mostly because he felt sorry for him. Shane had just moved from another city and didn't know anyone. Bradley had even invited Shane to his birthday party without being forced to by his mom. But that was my best friend for you. He was nice to everyone. It kind of made those of us with higher standards look bad.

"Hey," Bradley said brightly when he saw that I was still glaring at Shane, "people's parents will be here soon. We should play your game, Clara."

I glanced down at my digital precision wristwatch. Bradley was right. It was time for Chicken Chuckle Challenge—a fast-paced, laugh-out-loud-funny party game with an unexpected twist. I'd personally invented and planned it for Bradley's big day.

"Okay, everyone! Gather round." I stepped into the middle of the lawn. "Come on, Nelson, you too," I urged when Bradley's new friend still didn't put down his dull magazine.

I waited for him to join us and then I took a rubber chicken out of the bag of supplies I'd prepared and held it up over my head. "This," I explained, "is the Chuckle Chicken. The person holding it steps into the middle of the circle. They've got thirty seconds to do something that makes people laugh. Smiling doesn't count, but if even one person chuckles or giggles, they get to move on to the next round for a chance at the grand prize. And if nobody laughs ..." I trailed off ominously. I took out a paper bag and held it up in my other hand. (Here was the unexpected twist.) "… The person has to reach into the Bag of Doom and choose a dare."

"Oooooh!" Abby squealed. "I love dares."

"What's the grand prize?" Jamila asked.

"The grand prize," I said grandly as I dropped the other stuff on the grass and produced it from my pocket, "is this crisp five-dollar bill!" I held it by both ends and gave the bill a good snap.

"Can I go first?" asked Glenn, a boy who'd been in Ms. Smith's class with us. I nodded and he picked up the chicken. But even before the game could begin, Nelson started shaking his head and backing out of the circle.

"I'm not really into party games," he said.

I stared at him like he had three heads. I mean, party games are the best! Plus—not to brag— Chicken Chuckle Challenge was destined to become a classic.

Ten Reasons Why CHICKEN CHUCKLE CHALLENGE is an —INSTANT CLASSIC—

REASONS 1-10: It's a rubber chicken.
Need I say more?

I almost couldn't help myself. "Who doesn't like party games?" I asked out loud.

Nelson looked down at his sandals and gave an embarrassed smile, which was probably why Bradley answered for him. "Nelson's eleven," he said, as if that was any kind of explanation.

"It sounds fun and everything," Nelson added for himself. "But I think I'm just going to look at Bradley's new metal detector instead."

"Are you sure?" Bradley asked.

"Yeah, I'm sure," Nelson answered.

"Okay, then ... I'll come with you," Bradley offered. "We can even start putting it together if you want. I'll play the chicken game with you guys next time, okay?" he added when he saw the surprised look on my face.

"Are we ready?" Glenn asked. He was hugging the chicken to his chest and bouncing on the balls of his feet.

Bradley was already walking off with Nelson to the picnic table in the corner of the yard. And it wasn't like I could force the two of them to play if they didn't want to. I sighed, but I started the timer. Not surprisingly, hilariousness ensued.

Glenn got things off to a great start by pretending to sweep the chicken off its feet and kiss it. Jamila sat on the chicken: a surefire recipe for laughs. Then Abby did a wild, head-banging rock star routine. (The chicken was her electric guitar.) Each time someone went up, it got funnier and funnier ... and then it was my turn.

"Okay, guys. Get ready." I took the chicken from Abby. "This is going to be hilarious."

I leaned the chicken up against Bradley's crab-apple tree and then ran back to the other side of the yard and started the timer. I began my scene with a sound effect: a galloping noise that I made with my mouth as I pretended to hold the reins of a horse.

I stopped suddenly, like I'd just caught sight of the chicken. "Behold!" I said in my best British accent. "'Tis an adorable little chicken."

I glanced back at my audience. There were some smiles, but no laughs. At least, not yet.

"I shall approacheth." I galloped toward the chicken.

When I reached it, I pretended to dismount from my horse. "Oh hello, cuddly chicken," I said, picking it up gently. Then suddenly I made the chicken lunge at my throat. "Noooooo!" I cried out. "Aaaaaack! 'Tis a killer chicken! The foulest, cruelest chicken in the land." I dropped to the ground dead, letting my tongue fall out and rolling my eyes back in my head dramatically.

Once I was dead, I turned my head toward the party guests, awaiting their laughter and applause, only to be greeted by a strange, awkward silence.

"That was ... interesting ..." Jamila said.

But then—thankfully—just before my watch timer went off, I heard it: the sound of a familiar snort, coming from across the yard.

"That was so good," Bradley said. "Monty Python, right? The killer bunny skit? Only with a chicken!"

I nodded. Of course my best friend would appreciate my fresh take on a comedy classic.

Monty Python was an old British acting group. Bradley and I had spent many rainy afternoons watching their movies with my dad.

"What kind of a python?" Abby asked.

"I'll show you their videos next time you're at my house," I promised. I got up from the grass and passed the chicken over to Shane, who was supposed to be up next.

"Wait a sec," he said. "Nobody laughed. Doesn't that mean Clara has to do a dare?"

"Bradley laughed," Jamila pointed out.

"Yeah, but Bradley's not playing, is he?" Shane sneered. He grabbed the Bag of Doom and shoved it right in my face. "Go ahead," he said.

"No way!" I protested.

"Why not?" Shane countered. "You chicken or something?" He held up the rubber chicken. *"Bawk bawk bawk baaaawk."* That was the last straw.

"Fine!" I said. "I'll do a dare." It wasn't that big of a deal anyway. I'd written them myself, so I knew they weren't that bad.

But the second I saw the scrap of paper I'd pulled

out, I regretted giving in. "Suck your big toe for ten seconds," I read aloud. I'd kind of forgotten about that one.

"Oooooh," Abby winced.

"Gross!" Jamila added.

"Ha!" Shane said heartlessly.

I groaned. It was just my luck too ... I hadn't had a bath in at least three days. But then again, nobody calls Clara Humble chicken. Backing down wasn't an option.

I kicked off my flip-flop, sat down on the grass, and did what I had to do. But I couldn't help noticing that, even as I was busy sucking—and Shane, Jamila, Glenn, and Abby were counting down from ten—instead of cheering me on, Bradley had gone back to assembling the metal detector with Nelson. And if there was one thing worse than the taste of my own toe, it was the empty way that made me feel.

23

The Creepy Churchyard

Bradley's mom outdid herself with the loot bags. Not only did mine contain a huge lollipop and a keychain shaped like a globe, it also had an invisible-ink pen that only revealed your secret message when you shone a special light on it. Normally, I would have run to show my parents ... but I was in a truly terrible mood about how the chicken game had gone down. All I wanted was to be alone. Unfortunately, when I slid through the gap between my fence and Bradley's, my dad was standing in the middle of our yard.

"Uh-oh," he said when he noticed the look on my face. "You didn't win Pin the Tail on the Donkey?"

I grumbled, but that only made him do that annoying thing where he keeps trying to make me laugh. "No, wait ... You were playing Freeze Dance and your face got stuck like that?"

"Dad," I said, giving him a warning look.

"Okay, okay," he said. "You don't need to tell me what's wrong. But could you help me for a second?"

He was holding a tape measure. It was my favorite kind—with the long tongue that sticks out and then sucks back in when you press a button.

"Grab the end. I'm double-checking how much lumber I'll need for the new deck."

Ever since my dad had gotten a part-time job at H&H hardware, he'd been using his employee discount to make improvements around the house—and I'd been helping. (Measuring, sanding, and holding stuff steady were my areas of expertise.) We'd already built shelves to organize the garage and a panel that flipped out to reveal a foldaway ironing board in the laundry room. (It was a bit like those bookcases in haunted houses that flip around to reveal a secret passage, only way less exciting.)

But the new deck was going to be his pièce de résistance. (That's French for "thing he was going to brag about the most.") He'd been planning it since the winter and had already pre-invited h the neighbors for barbecues.

"Let's start up here," Dad said. "Right to the edge of the house." I already knew that we were measuring for the first tier: the cooking and food-prep zone. My dad had his eye on a GrillMaster Legend Four-Burner Gas BBQ with JetFire Ignition. Apparently, it could cook a steak medium-rare in thirty seconds flat.

THE GRILLMASTER LEGEND
For Men Who Live to Grill

100% macho or your money back.

I held my end as my dad backed across the yard, and once we were busy doing something, the words kind of jumped out.

"Bradley sort of hurt my feelings at the party," I found myself saying.

"He did?" Dad wrote a measurement on his notepad.

"He invited his new friend—Nelson, from JTT camp—and he mostly only hung out with him. He didn't even want to play the chicken game."

"But you worked so hard on that game!" Dad looked shocked, and he sounded almost as hurt as I'd been.

I nodded, already starting to feel a little better. My dad usually understood stuff like this.

"I'm sorry that happened. I wonder, though ..." he went on as he motioned for me to walk around so we could measure in the other direction. "If Bradley had a new friend over, maybe he was trying to make him feel extra-welcome. Everyone else at the party was from school, right?"

I'd been so busy thinking about what a drag Nelson was that I hadn't really considered that.

"It'd be like when you went to Claymation Kids last week," Dad explained.

The first day of Claymation Kids had been really hard. When Bradley and I had been looking at different summer camps, at first I'd tried to convince him to sign up for one called Cuddly Creatures with me.

"Look at this!" I'd said, clicking the link, which had the most adorable picture of a ferret wearing a camp hat. "You get to learn about taking care of animals—from cats to cattle."

Bradley had wrinkled his nose at the suggestion, just like I'd wrinkled mine at the idea of JTT. "I dunno. Remember when that caterpillar bit me last week? I'm not so great with animals. That's more your thing."

This was true. I happened to have a deep connection—some might say a psychic bond—with creatures great and small.

Once, a sparrow landed on my shoulder during a barbecue and tried to eat part of my hotdog bun. I let him have a piece and I swear he winked at me like we were best buds. Then when a traveling reptile exhibit came to school, guess whose shoe the salamander pooped on—twice? It might sound gross, but I consider it a sign of trust. You've got to be pretty relaxed to let go like that. I've even trained Bijou, my pet chinchilla, to do three

different tricks by rewarding her with raisins.
Plus, I'd been writing comics about @Cat—a hero
with the brains of a supercomputer and the heart
of a house cat—since I was seven. I just intuitively
understood what made her tick. (And I'm not only
talking about her billion-megawatt processor.)

Cuddly Creatures Camp was my kind of summer
fun. And I found out that Abby was already
registered, so even after Bradley said no, I was still
going to have a friend there.

Then disaster struck. By the time my dad
remembered to sign me up, Cuddly Creatures was
full. I ended up doing Claymation Kids for the first
week of summer instead. I was disappointed at
first, not to mention nervous.

Normally, I'm pretty good at making friends,
but everyone knew each other from after-school
lessons at the animation studio. Thankfully, this
girl Amanda sat with me at lunch and talked to me
at breaks. She even did the voice-over for Poodle
Noodle, the villainous balloon-animal poodle in
the film I made—@Cat: The Movie.

Yes, you heard that right! @Cat had made the
leap from the pages of comic books to the big

screen! During my week at Claymation Kids, I'd learned how to storyboard (plan out each scene on paper), build clay models, film, and even edit my very own movie. It was only twenty-three seconds long, but it was just the beginning. @Cat was destined for Hollywood.

After talking with my dad, I felt a little better about what had happened at the party. He was probably right. Bradley was trying to make Nelson feel welcome. And the next morning, when I answered the door and saw Bradley standing on my porch, I pretty much forgot about the whole thing—at least for a while.

"Remember what today is?" Bradley asked, grinning. He was holding his new metal detector and wearing the bright-orange sunhat he'd got at JTT camp the week before.

"Umm ..." I honestly had no idea. "The day after your birthday?"

"Exactly!" Bradley exclaimed. "And you know what that means."

Of course! I could hardly believe I'd forgotten!

Bradley and I had been begging to be allowed to go to the park down the street by ourselves—without an adult—for months. Roger at school had been doing it for almost a year. He was even allowed to bring his seven-year-old sister with him. And Bradley's cousins, who were younger than us, could go, even though the park near their house was on the other side of a busy street. But Bradley's mom kept saying he had to wait until he was ten. And when I asked my parents, they said they'd be comfortable with me going—but not alone. I needed to be with a friend who was at least ten.

"Let me go ask my dad, okay?" I ran up the stairs, taking them two at a time, and then bounded back down with the good news.

"He said okay. As long as I'm home by eleven o'clock."

"This is going to be awesome," Bradley said. We started down the porch steps. "Nelson says you can find amazing stuff buried in the sand at playgrounds. Like old coins and jewelry. I might even find another ring!"

I rolled my eyes a little at the mere mention of Nelson, but thankfully Bradley didn't seem to notice. He was probably too busy daydreaming about the possibility of valuable jewels. The week before, Bradley had found his very first true-and-for-real treasure while metal detecting on the beach with JTT Camp. It was a sterling silver dolphin ring with a genuine diamond-chip eye. His counselor said it might be worth as much as a hundred dollars. And, according to Bradley,

Nelson was 90 percent sure it was antique.

"Oh. Hi, Clara. Hi, Bradley," a voice said just as we reached the end of my driveway.

I looked up to see Shane's mom, Janet, standing on her porch with a mega-huge cup of coffee.

"Where are you guys headed?"

Unwisely, Bradley told her.

"That sounds fun. Mind if Shane joins you? He'd love to get some fresh air."

"Sure, I guess," Bradley answered, with his ever-present friendly smile. Meanwhile, I tried not to groan. After all, it wasn't Bradley's fault. Shane's mom was asking, and there's no easy way to say no to someone's mom.

"Great!" Janet said. She called into the house for Shane, who appeared a minute later, looking like the last person on earth who'd love to get fresh air.

"Do I have to?" he whined.

"Fresh air is important," Janet said. "Plus, I have a deadline to meet."

Shane's mom drew pictures for kids' books—and she was really, really good at it. She also had many other talents—like doing that loud whistle where you put your fingers in your mouth, and baking the world's best banana bread. Despite the fact that she'd killed Momo's garden and given birth to Shane, I liked her a lot.

"I'll fold the laundry. Or unload the dishwasher," Shane pleaded. "Just don't make me go."

But Janet wanted him to do something wholesome, and she wasn't taking no for an answer.

"You'll have fun," she said. "Just let me grab you a hat and some sunscreen."

"Awesome!" Shane said sarcastically after Janet had left. "I was just about to level up and earn the Sword of Destruction in *Doomsday Apocalypse Three*. Thanks for ruining it."

"We're ruining it?!" I spat back. "For your information, we didn't choose to invite you. We'd rather go to the park by ourselves."

Bradley didn't say anything nice, so I knew even he was disappointed. After all, it was our very first time out alone. Having to drag Shane along was going to take all the fun out of it.

"Some snacks," Janet said, reappearing in the doorway with Shane's backpack—and a bottle of SPF 60. She handed Shane the backpack, and then blurped a puddle of sunscreen into her palm and tried to smear him with it.

"Mom!" he shouted. "Jeez!"

"Stick together for safety!" Janet said brightly after she'd transferred the sunscreen to Shane's hand. "And you've got your cell phone, right? Charged up? Call if you need anything."

Shane grumbled something as his mom closed the door. Then he stomped down the stairs, slathering his arms in sunscreen.

"Let's just go to the park and get this over with," he muttered.

"Oh, we're not going to the park," I said, giving him The Look.

While Janet had been fussing with snacks and sunscreen, I'd decided exactly how to get rid of

Shane. "We're going exploring," I said as I started to stride down the sidewalk. "At the abandoned churchyard." I spun on my heel to see Shane's reaction.

Just as I'd anticipated, instead of jumping at the chance to investigate the spookiest place in our neighborhood, Shane went pale. Like I said before: ZERO sense of adventure.

"But we're not allowed there," Bradley said. "There are signs."

It was true. There were signs.

There was also a tall chain-link fence around the whole property, but the last time I'd walked past with my dad, I'd noticed that one part of the fence had come loose. I was pretty sure that if you pulled it up, there'd be a gap just big enough for a kid to squeeze through.

"I'm not afraid of a few signs," I said ... and then I turned to look at Shane. "Are you?"

"Of course not." Shane puffed out his chest, but the way his hands were clenched into fists gave him away.

And, okay, I'd never admit this to Shane, but the "Beware of Dog" sign had me a little concerned (even though I'd never seen or heard a dog there). And I wasn't sure what "prosecuted" meant, but it sounded a bit like "executed"—and that wasn't good. Still, if someone as brave as me felt a little bit scared, I knew Shane would be terrified, and that was the whole point. If I could freak him out enough, he'd go running home. And then I'd have something to tease him about the next time he said my cat-shaped barrettes were babyish or called me Clara Dumble.

"Signs or no signs, we can't go there," Bradley said in a no-nonsense voice that reminded me of his mother. "I told my nanny, Svetlana, we'd be at the park—and you told your dad the same thing."

"It's fine," I countered. "The park's just a block from the churchyard. They're practically the same thing."

"No, they're not," Bradley answered. "And since I'm the one who's ten ..."

This time I gave Bradley The Look. First he and Nelson were too mature for Chicken Chuckle Challenge, and now this? I mean, yes, he was officially ten, but that didn't make him my babysitter! I was going to be ten too in less than two months.

"Well, it's true," he said. "And if we get caught going someplace else, we might never be allowed out alone again."

"The park's more fun anyway," Shane added, which is how I knew for sure that he really was terrified.

"Fine then ..." I said. "If you guys don't want to explore the churchyard, I'll go alone. But Janet just said to stick together for safety. So if you don't come with me, you're both breaking that rule."

Even as I said it, I knew it didn't exactly make sense. Technically, I was the one forcing them to break the rule—but it hardly mattered. I was 90 percent sure Shane was going to run home any second, and then Bradley and I could just go to the park as we'd planned.

I turned and walked off down the street ... but it wasn't long before I heard Bradley's and Shane's footsteps behind me.

And that was when I realized that my plan was about to backfire. Shane didn't like the idea of sneaking into the abandoned churchyard one bit, but he was even more worried about me calling him a chicken. And Bradley was way too responsible to let me go by myself.

So unless I could think of some way out of it, it looked like we were about to get prosecuted.

The Cat

Even though it was eleven in the morning on a day so sunny it made your eyes hurt, the abandoned churchyard had a haunted feeling.

The thick, tangled weeds climbed halfway up the chain-link fence, hiding the view inside, and where there were gaps through the growth, I could see empty cigarette packs, broken bottles, and candy wrappers littering the ground.

In the middle of the yard, the old stone church loomed like something out of a nightmare. The steeple was crumbling, most of the windows were boarded up, and the dark hole in the tower (where the church bell must have been once) had a shadowy look that made me think someone or something was lurking inside, watching—a hunchbacked witch maybe, or at least a few evil ravens.

I wouldn't have minded passing by and heading

to the park like we'd planned, but there was no way I was giving Shane Biggs the satisfaction. So instead, I took a deep breath and led the way, half a block past the locked gate to the broken part of the fence.

Once I'd checked that no one was coming down the street in either direction, I pulled back the chain-link to show Shane and Bradley the opening. "Go ahead," I told Shane.

He glanced up at the "Beware of Dog" sign and for a second I got my hopes up, but then he shoved his backpack through the hole and climbed in after it.

"Clara." Bradley fixed me with a stare. "This is a bad idea."

He sounded like my mom scolding me for wearing my spunky skunk T-shirt on picture day—when, hello, years from now, that's how everyone's going to remember me.

My fourth grade class photo.

"It'll be fine," I promised. "We'll only stay a few minutes. And it's totally safe. It's just a church, right?"

I'd been to Sunday school with Bradley before, and the most dangerous thing I'd seen there was a pair of safety scissors left on the rug in the preschool room. The people who owned the church had probably just put up the scary signs to keep vandals away ... and obviously we weren't there to do any damage.

"Anyway," I continued, "if you want treasure, this place is a million times better than the park. Look how ancient it is."

That got Bradley's attention. He squinted up at the worn-out building.

"It's got to be, what? A hundred years old?" I said.

I could practically see the possibilities swirling through his mind: rare coins, ancient religious relics, a huge diamond ring lost by a long-ago bride ... I lifted the fence and Bradley sighed softly, but he ducked through.

As soon as we were safely inside and past some of the tall weeds, Bradley seemed to relax a little.

Actually, so did I. Except for all the garbage and the total lack of lawn care, it wasn't so bad. The noises of the neighborhood seemed to fade away, and a bird or two twittered in the branches of a big tree.

I led the way toward a gravel pathway—the only spot that was mostly clear of weeds—and Bradley switched on his metal detector. It made a high-pitched static sound as he swept it back and forth over the ground.

"Do you have to do that?" Shane asked in a frantic whisper. "What if someone hears?"

"Stop worrying," I said. "No one's even around."

"You know, we're probably the first people to metal detect in here in years ... maybe ever," Bradley added. "We could easily find something valuable. My camp counselor said that last year one of his campers found a rare silver dollar in a flower bed near a church parking lot. And that was just the parking lot!"

Bradley adjusted a dial on his detector. "Did you know our whole neighborhood used to belong to a rich family named the Schneiders? It was an apple orchard. That was between the mid-1800s and the early 1920s, when they sold it all to the city."

As Bradley was talking, he was watching the ground, which was why he didn't notice Shane rolling his eyes and making his hand into a puppet that was going, "Blah, blah, blah." But I noticed it all right.

What Shane's hand would say if it had a will of its own.

If I wasn't so attached to it, I'd give my right arm to get away from this bozo!

By then we'd reached the church. It had a big chain and padlock on the front door, so I stepped off the pathway and into the tall weeds to check the doors around back. The boys followed.

"I don't know if I told you yet," Bradley said to Shane as we waded through the weeds, "but last week at JTT, I found a ring with a real diamond chip in it. And Nelson discovered a brass button that might have been from a military uniform. It was awesome. Actually, that's where I got this cool hat." He took off his bright-orange hat and pointed out the logo on the front to Shane.

I crouched down and tried to peer through a basement window, but the glass was all cloudy, and it was pitch-black inside.

"I'm going back the first week of August," Bradley continued. "There might still be space. You could ask your mom to sign you up if you want."

"Uh, no thanks," Shane said rudely. Then he added under his breath, "Sounds laaaaame."

Now, like I said before, Junior Treasure Trackers wasn't exactly my thing either, but that didn't make it "laaaaame." And nobody gets to make fun of my best friend ... well, except for me—and I only ever do it in a nice way, and only when he does stuff like insist on eating the noodles in his alphabet soup in alphabetical order, because c'mon.

And that was why—even though I knew Shane was following me closely—as I walked behind the church, I didn't bother warning him about the big plank of wood in the tall grass that I'd just noticed and stepped right over.

"What the—?" Shane tripped and then stumbled past me, falling through the waist-high weeds. "Oof!" His hands flew out to break his fall and made contact with what looked like a low wooden fence at first ... but then his knees came down on another part of it, and the weeds parted, revealing a park bench.

"Ouch." He rubbed at one knee. "Clara! You could've told me to watch out!"

But I wasn't paying attention to him. I'd just caught a glimpse of something golden.

"Move over." I kneeled down beside Shane and yanked up some of the tall weeds, throwing them over my shoulder. "Look," I whispered. I rubbed my finger over the plaque that had just been uncovered. "It's a dead-person bench!"

Bradley switched off the metal detector, stepped over the big wooden board, and came to take a look. "It is a dead-person bench!" The little golden plaque read: *In Memory of John Nichols: Forever in Our Hearts. 1931–2005.* "Do you think he's buried underneath it?" Bradley asked in a whisper.

I doubted it, but it seemed like a good chance to scare Shane. "It's possible." I made my eyes go wide. "Dead people get buried in churchyards all the time, right?"

I leaned forward, meaning to rub the tarnish off the plaque with the bottom of my T-shirt, but as my weight shifted, the bench rocked on the uneven ground.

"Oh my God!" Shane leaped up and stumbled backward. He landed on the ground on his bum.

"Oh no, Shane!" I gasped before grinning. "That was the ghost of Old John Nichols! We've angered him, and now he's rocking the bench. Wooo!" I wailed as I shifted my weight to tip the bench from side to side. "Wooooo!"

"Oh, shut up, Clara." Shane got to his feet and brushed himself off, but I noticed that he kept a safe distance from the bench. "We saw the churchyard, okay? Can we go?"

"But we haven't even really explored yet," I pointed out.

"The doors are locked. There's nothing interesting."

We still needed to check the basement windows, though. Maybe one would be open. Except I never got around to suggesting it because, just then, we heard it: something undeniably interesting, not to mention truly terrifying.

YEEEEEEEOOOOOW.

"What was that?!" I barely remembered leaping

to my feet, but I found myself standing way back from the dead-guy bench, clutching Bradley's arm.

The strange shrieking noise that had pierced the air was somewhere between the scratching of fingernails on a chalkboard and the sound the air makes when you let it out through the pinched end of a balloon. It was ghastly and grating—ghostly even.

"Dunno," Shane said, "and I'm not staying to find out." He crashed through the weeds, jumped over the fallen plank, and ran past the church and straight toward the gap in the fence, leaving me and Bradley behind.

Maybe we were frozen to the spot with fear, or perhaps our curiosity got the best of us, because neither of us moved ... and then the noise came again. This time, because it didn't take us by surprise, we could hear it more clearly.

YEEEEEEEOOOOOW.

Suddenly, I knew it was no ghost. I stepped forward, crouched down, and peered under the bench.

"Bradley!" I said, laughing. "It's just a little cat!"
The cat was mostly white, with brown and

gray patches—including one around its eye that was shaped almost like a heart. It had super-soft-looking fur and extra-wispy whiskers.

"Hey, little kitty," I cooed.

Ferocious, terrifying kitty cat.

I reached under the bench to pet it, but instead of sniffing me and then rubbing its cheek against my hand like Momo's cats used to do, this one bared its fangs and hissed. It backed away and then started to make the screeching sound again. It did it three or four times, before lying down on its side and panting.

"Bradley," I said, looking over my shoulder. "It seems dehydrated. Check if Shane's mom packed him any water."

Luckily, Shane had dropped his backpack on the ground near the bench before he ran out. Bradley unzipped it and handed me a water bottle and a stick of string cheese. "In case the cat's hungry," he explained. "Although from the looks of it, it's pretty well-fed."

49

For such a small cat, it did have a surprisingly round belly.

"Don't try to touch her, okay?" I warned. (I'd already figured out that the cat was probably a "she" because of her pretty face and delicate paws.) "She's really scared. We're going to have to earn her trust."

I opened Shane's water bottle and poured some water into the cap. The cat waited until I'd backed away before very cautiously inching over and starting to lap at the water.

"That's it, little kitty," I said softly.

But even though my voice normally had an extremely soothing effect on animals (especially Bijou, my pet chinchilla, who always came out of the Kleenex box I kept in her cage when I called), the cat stopped drinking, looked up, and hissed again.

"I think she likes you," Bradley joked.

"Of course she likes me," I answered. "She's just spooked. Who knows how long she's been in this churchyard all alone." I opened the string-cheese package, pulled a strip off, and set it down beside the water dish, but she didn't even sniff it.

Instead, the cat started to circle on the spot, making the yowling noise again. It wasn't normal feline behavior. Something was wrong: I just knew it.

@Cat: Demonstrating Some (Mostly) Normal Feline Behavior

Sleeping in sunny spots.

Lounging in inconvenient places.

Refueling after a busy day.

"I think she might be sick."

"Maybe we should take her to a vet," Bradley suggested.

I bit at my fingernails while I considered this. I knew from Momo that taking a cat to the vet cost a fortune. Plus, we'd need someone to drive us. But my dad had to leave for his shift at the hardware store at noon, Bradley's mom was at work, and Svetlana didn't like animals much. (We'd learned that the hard way the time we found a toad in Bradley's backyard and built it a habitat in the kitchen sink.)

What's more, a few months before, when Bradley and I had found and tried to rescue a stray animal (a baby raccoon that had its head stuck inside a peanut butter jar), things hadn't turned out well …

Like I said before, I've always shared a special bond with animals. Plus, I'd watched enough *Crocodile Wrestler* to pretty much know what I was doing. But Bradley's mom had walked outside just as we'd been busy wrapping the raccoon's back end in a towel so we could try to pull the jar loose. And after she was done yelling about the danger of rabies, the importance of making good choices, and why the white towels with embroidered edges were only for guests, she'd called Animal Services. A man with a ponytail and a woman with an even longer ponytail had shown up in a big white van and taken the raccoon far away, never to be seen in our neighborhood again.

"If we ask our parents to take her to the vet, they'll probably just send her away instead," I pointed out. "Remember Skippy?" We still talked about that peanut butter raccoon often, and wondered how he was doing.

Bradley nodded solemnly. He pushed the string cheese a little closer to the cat.

"Unless ..." I said, getting an idea.

"Unless what?" he asked.

"Unless we can convince our parents to let us adopt her."

I knew it wouldn't be easy. I'd put "cat" at the top of every birthday and Christmas list for as long as I could remember—but my parents always said one chinchilla was more than enough pet. Bradley had asked for a pet a few times too, but his mom had nice furniture and she didn't want it scratched or peed on.

Still, it couldn't hurt to try again, could it?

"I mean, as long as we don't specifically tell them that the cat we want to adopt is living in the churchyard ..." I reasoned.

"Then even if they say no to a cat, they won't know this one exists." Bradley finished my thought.

I glanced at my watch. It was 10:55. We needed to head home.

Bradley and I both stood up and started through the weeds. "Whatever you do, don't tell Shane we found a cat, okay?" I said. "He'll only tattle on us."

Bradley nodded.

"In fact, don't tell anyone." I took another step, and then I stopped. "Just a sec." I ran back and crouched in front of the bench. I needed to see her one last time before we went. "Don't worry, kitty," I said softly. "We'll be back soon to take care of you and hopefully bring you home."

"YEEEEEEOOOOOW," the cat screeched in response. She puffed up her tail and hissed, but I didn't mind. She was feisty, and I liked that in a feline. She was also the prettiest cat in the whole wide world. I already knew there was nothing I wouldn't do for her.

The Begging and Pleading Begins

My dad was working afternoons at the hardware store that week, which meant I was heading to Bradley's after lunch so Svetlana could look after me. As soon as I arrived, we got to work researching and making a list of six indisputable reasons why getting a cat was a great idea. Plus, we worked out a detailed pet co-ownership schedule in case both our parents said yes. By the time I headed home, I was mentally exhausted but thoroughly prepared.

Because I'm a master of strategy, I waited for the right moment to make my proposal: after my parents had eaten dinner and had time to relax, but before they turned on the *News at 6* and decided the world was basically doomed. It was a ten-minute window.

"Hey," I said, ever-so-casually, as I flopped down

on the couch between my mom and dad. "I've been thinking ... wouldn't it be great to get a cat?"

Mom lowered the book she'd been reading and locked eyes with my father. She gave him a small smile that said "Oh no" and "Here we go again," but I didn't let it discourage me.

"For one thing," I started, "owning a pet is a great way to learn responsibility."

"Well then," Dad said, "good thing you've already got a pet."

"Which reminds me," Mom added. "You haven't cleaned Bijou's cage yet this week, have you?"

I'd been meaning to. It was just that one of my summer goals was to teach my chinchilla to break dance. We were working on a tailspin kind of move. She was so close to nailing it, and B-girling was more fun than cleaning up stinky wood chips. "Not yet," I admitted. "But if we had a cat, I'd definitely clean Bijou's cage without being reminded."

"How do you figure that?" Mom asked.

"Because, like I said, I'd be learning so much responsibility." My parents didn't look convinced, so I pressed on. "Anyway, did you know that cats are total neat freaks? They're practically self-cleaning!"

"Except for the litter box," Dad pointed out. "And when they cough up hairballs on the rug."

"Well, yeah." I'd never personally heard of a cat—even a super-intelligent one—that was willing to scoop out its own litter box or clean up its own hairballs. In fact, the more intelligent a cat was, the less likely it was that it would stoop so low.

"Sure, you have to clean the litter box." I moved seamlessly to my next point. "But cats more than make up for it by keeping pests, like rats and mice, out of your home."

"That would be a huge help," Mom conceded, "... if we had any rats or mice."

Cleaning the litter box is one of the many menial tasks that @Cat delegates to the human.

"We do have a chinchilla, though. I'm not sure Bijou would appreciate sharing the house with a cat," Dad pointed out. "What if it tried to hunt her?"

Chinchillas are rodents, like rats and mice, but I was almost positive I could train Bijou and the cat to be friends. I'd seen plenty of internet videos showing interspecies friendships: an owl and a possum that liked to play tag, a pig that let a monkey ride on its back ... even a dog cuddling with a giant lizard.

I glanced at the clock. I was running out of time. I needed to pull out the most indisputable of the indisputable reasons: numbers four, five, and six—which were all related to health and safety. Parents love health and safety.

"Also, playing with a cat can be great exercise," I pointed out. "And cats have been shown to decrease stress. In fact, some people believe their purring has healing powers. And finally," I paused to give my big conclusion more impact, "in the event of a fire, a cat might save our lives."

My mom actually laughed, which I thought was rude and unnecessary.

"It's true!" I cried. "I read about it in a library book! There was this cat called Pookie in Australia. She saved an entire family from a fire by meowing until they woke up."

"Well, I'm glad Pookie was such a hero, Clara. But we check our smoke alarms regularly, so you don't need to worry."

I couldn't help it. I groaned in frustration.

"Look, Clara," Dad said. "We've talked about this before. You already know our answer."

"One chinchilla is—" Mom started, but she didn't need to finish her sentence.

"Yeah, yeah," I said. "More than enough pet."

My dad picked up the remote and switched on the TV.

I stomped up the stairs. It figured! I'd just presented my parents with six research-backed reasons to get a cat, and they'd barely listened.

But all news anchor Kai Zhou had to do was say a few ridiculous words about sharks and they were all ears. When, hello! Any friend to animals (or anyone who's ever watched Shark Week on the Discovery Channel) knows that sharks are an important and often misunderstood part of the ocean ecosystem who need our protection.

Well, if they thought I was going to give up that easily, they didn't know me very well. And in the meantime, I'd just have to hope (for the cat's sake) that Bradley's mom had been more reasonable.

After I fed Bijou—and we'd got down to a few funky beats—I went next door to find out, but Bradley wasn't in his yard or inside. (I knocked on both doors and peered through the windows.) At first, I figured he was running errands with his mom, but I waited half an hour and they still weren't back. It wasn't until the next morning that I found out why.

"Where were you last night?!" I said as soon as I'd wiggled through the gap between my fence and his. Bradley was sitting on his porch steps reading a book. "We needed to talk about the cat," I added in an urgent whisper, glancing toward the back windows, which were partly open.

"I know." Bradley marked his place with a bookmark. "Sorry! We ran into Nelson's family at the grocery store and his mom is so nice that she invited us for a barbecue. Like, that very same night! I couldn't say no without raising suspicions."

"Oh," I said. "Really?" I didn't want to make him feel bad, but I was kind of disappointed. He could have thought of some way out of it. Like faking the flu ... or saying he had to do an important advanced homework assignment for fifth grade. I mean, our cat needed us!

I couldn't stay mad for long, though, because these were the very next words out of Bradley's mouth: "Do you think she's okay?" He bit his lip anxiously. Then he flipped his book open again. "I've been reading about cat diseases, but none of the symptoms seem to match hers."

"Where'd you get that?" I asked, eyeing the book.

"Nelson loaned it to me," Bradley answered.

"Nelson has a cat?" I never would have guessed. Probably because it was hard to imagine someone so serious running around the house with a piece of string, making up cute nicknames, or spending a lazy cat-urday afternoon curled up on the couch giving ear scratches.

"Two, actually," Bradley answered. "They're both Persians. Their names are Rembrandt and Maximilian."

Now, I love all animals, but Persians are the snobbiest breed of cat. Everyone knows that. And Rembrandt and Maximilian? Could you get any more show-offy than those names?

"Wait!" I said, suddenly feeling panicky. "You didn't tell Nelson about our cat, did you? We agreed not to tell anyone."

"Of course not," Bradley reassured me. "I just told him I was thinking about getting one."

"And?" I said. He didn't need to ask what I meant.

"My mom didn't even let me get past the second of the six indisputable reasons," he said sadly.

Then he had to shout the next part to be heard over the sawing noises coming from my yard. The forecast was calling for rain, and my dad was determined to finish the support beams for the first tier of the deck before noon. "She said that— even if it didn't scratch the furniture—Stuart's allergic, so end of discussion."

Stuart was Bradley's mom's boyfriend. He only lived at their house on the weekends, so it was beyond unfair that Bradley wasn't allowed to have a cat because of him.

"What did your mom and dad say?" Bradley asked, but I think he already knew the answer from the look on my face.

Finally my dad stopped sawing. In the sudden quiet, Bradley and I both sighed.

"I'm definitely asking again," I said. "They can't say no forever, can they?"

Bradley nodded somberly. "I'll ask again too," he said. "But in the meantime, we're going to need to look after the cat in secret. That's why I borrowed this book from Nelson."

He consulted the table of contents and then flipped some pages. "It says here that an adult cat needs about 240 calories a day. Plus plenty of fresh, clean water."

I didn't want to make Bradley feel bad, so I didn't say this out loud, but we didn't really need Nelson's book. Since Momo had cats, I'd basically grown up with felines.

"Cats are also carnivores, so they need lots of

protein," Bradley said, still skimming the book. "The best thing to feed them is a high-quality cat food specially formulated for their dietary needs."

"Mm-hmm." I picked some dirt out from under my fingernails. Cats eat cat food. This was pretty basic stuff. Plus, at the moment, I had a more important issue on my mind. "I was thinking," I said. "We can't keep calling her 'the cat.' She needs a real name."

Bradley finally put the book down. "I was thinking that too. What about Spike?"

Spike? It was better than Maximilian, but of all the possible cat names, there couldn't be one less right for our petite, precious kitty. "I was thinking more along the lines of Isadorabella." I said it in a floaty, dreamy kind of voice because it was a floaty, dreamy kind of name.

Bradley frowned. "Isn't that a little ..." he paused, looking for the right word, "long?"

"Braaaaadley!" Svetlana called out the back window. "We're making sassy shakers now!"

I tilted my head and narrowed my eyes in a question.

"Toilet paper rolls with rice in them," Bradley explained. "It's one of my sister Val's baby crafts."

"Can me and Clara go to the park instead?" he called back.

"Sure," Svetlana answered. "If it's okay with Clara's dad. But come straight home if the sky gets darker, okay? And no talking to strangers," she added. "Unless you need help in an emergency. Then only talk to familiar strangers."

Bradley and I looked at each other and shrugged.

"Okay," he yelled. Then we checked with my dad and we were on our way.

On a hot summer's day in our neighborhood, the Corner Milk 'n' Variety is the place to see and be seen—and also, you know, to buy bread and stuff. When Bradley and I arrived, the bench out front was already filled with sixth graders from our school. They were all eating popsicles. I waved to them casually as we walked past, but inside I felt a little thrill. Finally, Bradley and I had joined their ranks—cruising the neighborhood alone like wild coyotes or bored teenagers.

Andy, the store's owner, looked up from the magazine he'd been reading when he saw us come in.

"There are my favorite customers." When he smiled, his face wrinkled like a damp paper bag. "No mom or dad today?" he asked.

"Nah," I answered, like it was no big deal. "We're nearly in fifth grade now."

"Well, imagine that. Growing up, eh?"

Andy had known me and Bradley since we were babies. Actually, Andy knew everyone in the neighborhood because he'd been running the corner store forever. (I wouldn't have been surprised to learn he'd been born there.) He used to work the cash while his wife, Claudette, stocked the shelves, but she died the year before, so now it was just Andy. Sometimes I wondered if he was sad, but it was hard to tell. He always acted happy when he saw me, and he was always prepared.

"I've got a good one for you today," he said. "Nearly impossible!"

The riddle thing had started on a particularly boring rainy afternoon when I'd walked over with my dad to buy raisin bread. "What can I getcha?" Andy had asked us. But that day, instead of telling him, I gave him clues and made him guess. He must have been having a pretty dull afternoon too, because he really got into it.

THE RAISIN-BREAD RIDDLE:
What do you get when bread and fruit make a toast?

UMMM ... Grainy juice?

soggy bread?

His eyes twinkled in anticipation as he leaned forward. "What can travel around the world without leaving the corner?" He tapped the counter once and then sat back.

I stared at the shiny lottery tickets on display while I let my mind go to work. An airplane, suitcases, important businesspeople: They all traveled. But the only things I could think of that stayed in a corner were potted plants, L-shaped bookshelves, and umbrella stands—and they weren't known for their globe-trotting ways.

Andy grinned. He could tell he had me. I looked to Bradley, but he only shrugged.

"Mull it over," Andy said. "Maybe this will help you think." He slid a box out from behind the counter. Cherry Twizzlers. "Fresh in today."

Bradley and I each took a few and Andy held open a paper bag for us to put them in. We tried to pay, but he waved our money away. "Put it in your piggy banks," he said. "What I will take is another one of those cat movies, if you've got one."

The last time I'd been in with my mom to buy milk, I'd borrowed her cell phone so I could show Andy @*Cat: The Movie*. He'd always been a fan of my comic strip, so I knew he'd like it, but I hadn't realized just how much. He even got up from his stool to give it a standing ovation. Unfortunately, though, I was still no closer to coming up with an idea for the sequel I wanted to make.

"Sorry," I said. "I'm still in the planning stages."

"Ah. You can't rush genius." Andy winked. "So," he went on. "What can I getcha today? Some refreshing popsicles? Milk for mom or dad?"

"Actually," I said, leaning against the counter and lowering my voice, "we need a bag of your finest-quality cat food."

Andy raised his eyebrows, but he didn't ask questions. He was used to selling strange things: whipped cream and bologna, toilet paper and Tootsie Rolls, a jar of pickles and some cookie-dough ice cream at midnight. Cat food for two kids who'd never mentioned owning a cat before was no big deal. "Let's see what we've got."

He led us to a back corner of the store. It was an area I'd never been in before—past the potato chip racks, canned soups, and cleaning products—right near the door to the storage room. It was dark, and the floor was slightly sticky. "Here you go," Andy said. "We've got two brands to choose from."

I picked up the closest bag and handed it to Bradley. It was coated in a fine layer of dust that made him sneeze almost immediately.

"Gesundheit," Andy said. It was his way of saying "Sorry you sneezed."

"Thanks." Bradley turned the bag around to read the label. "This one's got 242 calories a serving," he said, "which is just about right."

I lifted the other bag off the shelf. You could tell it was a higher-quality food—mostly because the bag was a vibrant orange, and the cat on it looked sportier. Also, it was called Opti-1 Feline Nutrition Formula, which sounded really scientific.

"We'll take this one," I said to Andy. After all, Isadorabella deserved the best.

"All righty, then." Andy carried it up to the cash and rang it in. "That'll be ten ninety-nine."

I turned to Bradley with a little shrug. If I'd known we were going to find a cat, I would have saved up, but I'd already taken an advance on my allowance for the rest of the summer to buy

Claymation supplies.

"I'll pay next time," I promised. Bradley frowned a little, but he dug around in his pockets. "I've only got nine dollars and fifty cents," he said. "Why don't we just get the first brand? It's cheaper and just as healthy."

"But this one has meaty gourmet flavors," I pointed out.

"That's all right," Andy said. "Nine fifty is close enough. Pay me the rest next time you come in, okay?"

"Okay," I said. "Thanks, Andy!"

But Bradley looked uneasy. At first I thought it was because he didn't like the idea of owing Andy money—and that might have been part of it—but then I followed his gaze. He was staring out the door at someone coming in: Shane Biggs, to be exact. I grabbed the cat food and, quick as a flash, shoved it under my T-shirt ... which unfortunately was a little bit see-through when you stretched it that much.

"Why are you carrying cat food under your shirt, Clara?" Shane asked, scowling at me.

I said the first thing that popped into my head. "I'm conserving plastic bags."

He narrowed his eyes. "You don't even have a cat," he said.

I drew a blank. In their ongoing quest to be neighborly, my parents had invited Shane and his mom over for apricot cobbler just two weeks before. Shane had barely touched his (a colossal waste of cobbler!). Then my mom said I should show him Bijou. And even though I got her to do her best trick (climbing the curtains), he'd acted bored and asked if I had any better pets ... and of course, I'd said no.

Thankfully, Bradley came to the rescue. "It's for my mom's boyfriend's cat," he lied. "We're taking care of her. She's a Russian Blue."

"A blue cat?" Shane scoffed.

"That's just the name of the breed. Russian Blues are actually gray. They've also got a double coat of fur and pleasant personalities." This must have been yet another fact from *Felines for Fools*.

"Fascinating," Shane said flatly. Then he pushed past us to get to the freezer. "But I came for a cherry popsicle, not a lecture on cats."

"Don't mind him," I said to Bradley—but loudly, so Shane would be sure to overhear, even with his head stuck inside the freezer. "He doesn't know the first thing about what's interesting. All he does is play video games."

Shane emerged from the freezer to glare at me, but I just hugged the cat food more tightly to my stomach and turned on my heel.

We waved goodbye to Andy, pushed the door open, and walked out, leaving the shop bells ringing behind us.

But before I could storm off down the sidewalk, something stopped me in my tracks. My eyes had landed on the red mailbox on the corner. Suddenly, I knew the answer to Andy's nearly impossible riddle!

"One sec," I called over my shoulder to a baffled Bradley. I ran back and pulled the door open. "A stamp!" I shouted to Andy over the jangling of the shop bells. "You put it in the corner of your letter, and it travels around the world."

"You got it," he said, giving me a thumbs-up. "I knew you would."

The Kittens

We love and cuddle our pets. We call them adorable names. But it's important to remember: As much as they're like family members, they're also creatures with strong animal instincts.

Even @Cat—who can be as civilized as she is technologically advanced—has her moments of pure cattiness.

Which explains why when I saw

The time @Cat rescued Mother Robin's babies from danger. Well ... mostly.

Oops!

what Isadorabella was up to that morning, as grossed out as I was, my first thought was that she was only doing what cats are born to do.

"Yuck! She caught a whole bunch of mice," I called out to Bradley. I'd run across the churchyard ahead of him so I could be the first to peer under the bench. The cat was licking the tiny, wiggling creatures like she wanted them spick-and-span for her supper.

"Stop that." I poked her gently with a stick. Even though I understood that cats had hunting instincts, as a friend to all animals, I couldn't let her get away with mouse murder. And anyway, she didn't need to hunt anymore. Not when she had us to feed her.

Izzy-B (as I'd decided to call her for short) seemed to disagree, though. She swatted at my stick and went right back to cleaning her food. I sighed, took a deep breath, and then reached in to rescue the mice. But even before I'd touched a single one, she hissed and snapped at my hand. I only just managed to pull it away without getting bitten.

Bradley crouched down beside me. "Wait a sec." He unzipped his backpack. "I don't think those are mice." He opened Nelson's copy of *Felines for Fools* and flipped through it. "Here." He showed me a page with the heading "Kitten Development." At the bottom, it had pictures of adorable, fluffy kittens playing with balls of yarn, but as I followed the pictures up the page, the kittens became less and less cute. In the first photo, they had wet fur, pinkish-gray skin, flat ears, squinted-shut eyes, and naked tails. They looked more like hairless gerbils from outer space than kittens.

Just then, one of the tiny creatures opened its mouth and a frail mewing noise escaped.

"No way!" I gasped.

"Spike's a mommy," Bradley said in wonder. "How many are there?"

It was hard to tell. The kittens were piled in a heap against their mother's belly. They were also wriggling and weaving their heads from side to side as they searched for a place to nurse.

"Five, I think." I squinted at the pile. "No, wait." There was a tiny one on the bottom. I could just see its little pink nose. "Six."

Everything made perfect sense now! When the cat had been walking around in circles and yowling, she hadn't been sick. She'd been getting ready to have her babies.

"Pass me the food." I tore open the bag and dumped a pile of kibble on the ground.

Right away, the mother cat's nose went crazy. She nudged the kittens off and stood up. After casting a glance in our direction to be sure we weren't making any sudden moves, she approached the pile. But as soon as she'd taken her first bite, her hunger seemed to win out over her fear. She hunched down and crunched loudly.

While the mother cat ate and Bradley poured water into an old yogurt container we'd brought, I took the opportunity to get a little closer to the kittens. The ones I liked to watch in the pet store window at the mall were funny, fluffy, and rough-and-tumble. These kittens seemed so meek, with their pinched-up faces and rubbery-looking legs.

Bradley was watching them too. Then he looked up at the sky. "It's supposed to pour rain."

I could tell he was thinking what I was thinking: Would such helpless kittens survive a storm?

"We need to get them to shelter," I said.

"Yeah, but where?" Bradley asked. "If we're not allowed one cat at our houses, we're definitely not allowed seven."

"I'll sneak them into my room," I said.

Bradley cast a glance at the mother cat. "I have a feeling Spike wouldn't like us touching her kittens."

"You mean Isadorabella," I corrected. At the sound of her name, the cat stopped eating, looked over her shoulder, and hissed.

"She obviously prefers Spike," Bradley said with a smile. But even as we talked, the sky was starting to grow darker. It wasn't the time to be arguing about names—or the time to be reading, but Bradley was busy turning the pages of *Felines for Fools* again.

"It says here that the most important thing for kittens is to be with their mother. If you find stray kittens, you shouldn't move them unless you really have to."

I actually hadn't known that before, but I wasn't about to admit to Bradley that super-serious know-it-all Nelson's book had come in handy.

"We probably don't have time to move them anyway," I said. "We could build them a shelter here. At least for now."

Bradley nodded. "Only what will we build it out of?"

"Yeah. What will you build it out of?"

Bradley and I both jumped at the sound of the voice. We'd been so focused on the kittens that we hadn't even heard Shane Biggs tiptoeing through the weeds. He must have followed us all the way from Andy's Milk 'n' Variety. How long had he been leaning against the back wall of the church, listening in?

"I knew you were lying," he said to Bradley as he sauntered over. "Your mom's boyfriend doesn't have a blue cat."

"What business is it of yours anyway?" I challenged, shifting my body so I was between Shane and the kittens.

"If you're sneaking around taking care of dirty stray cats that probably have fleas, I think your parents would be very interested in that information. Especially since you're not even allowed at the churchyard in the first place."

As if sensing Shane's hostility, the mother cat abandoned her kibble and tried to dash back to her kittens. But when she saw me crouched in the way, instead of understanding that I was protecting them from a real threat (Shane Biggs), she must have thought I was trying to keep her from her babies—and, like any good mother, she was willing to fight for her young.

It started with a low growl in her throat, and then her tail puffed and she arched her back. Her fur stood on end.

"Clara," Bradley warned. "I think you'd better get out of Spike's way."

"Yeah," Shane added unhelpfully. "That thing's psycho."

But I wasn't afraid. I held up my hands to show Izzy-B that I meant no harm. "It's okay." I started shifting to the side to let her through, but before I knew what was happening, she lunged at me and swiped at my bare shin with her claws— right in the same spot where I already had a pretty impressive scab from falling off my bike the week before.

"Ow!" I said, leaping to my feet. I watched as Izzy-B dashed past me and came to a skidding stop. She crouched near her kittens, eyeing me while making another low noise in her throat.

"You're bleeding!" Bradley said, pointing to my leg. The scratch had made part of the old scab come off, and bright-red blood was trickling down my shin. "Are you okay?"

"Yeah, I'm fine," I answered bravely—even

though it hurt. "Don't worry about me." I glanced up at the sky. "Let's just build the shelter, okay?"

"You're still planning to go near that cat?" Shane said. "How dumb can you get? It probably has all kinds of diseases."

"You probably have all kinds of diseases," I countered. "Just go home, okay? We're busy assisting animals."

"And what's in it for me?" Shane asked, with a sneer that showed off his pink-popsicle-tinged teeth.

"What do you mean 'What's in it for me?'"

"I mean, if I don't tell on you, you need to make it worth my while."

Leave it to Shane to be thinking of himself when there were creatures in need! I should probably have known better than to negotiate with him, but just then there was a rumbling of thunder. The cat family needed shelter, and there was no time to waste.

"Here." I reached into my back pocket and pulled out the paper bag full of Twizzlers that Andy had given us. "Take them!"

Shane opened the bag and sniffed. "They're

fresh," he said, seeming satisfied. He took one out and bit the end off. "All right. I'll keep my mouth shut. For now."

"Great," I said. "Now get lost."

Shane bit off another piece of licorice and started toward the fence. "I'm going," he said over his shoulder. "But I'll be back. And when I am, there'd better be more candy."

Bradley looked surprised and a little disgusted. (I kept forgetting that he hadn't seen as much of Shane's meanness firsthand as I had.)

"What about that cardboard box that was over near the church?" I asked Bradley as Shane walked off. "We could flatten it out and wrap it around the legs of the bench to keep out the wind."

"Or put it on its side and try to scoop the kittens into it," Bradley said. "*Felines for Fools* says kittens like the coziness of a box."

"Okay," I said. "And we can tie plastic bags together and put them over the box to keep out the rain."

We set to work, scouring the churchyard for old bags, plastic packaging, and anything else we could use to make the shelter safe, dry, and warm. And even though it usually bugged me when people were litterbugs, for once I was glad.

By the time we tied on the last plastic bag, the first drops of rain were just starting to fall. Izzy-B approached the box and sniffed it. Once she decided it was safe, she began to lift the kittens by the scruff of the neck, one by one, and nestle them inside.

"She actually likes it," Bradley said with a smile.

"Let's just hope it does the trick," I said, adjusting the plastic bags so that they covered the opening most of the way.

The rain was off to a slow start—splashing us with a drop or two every few seconds—but judging by the dark clouds, it seemed likely to pour any minute. I knew my dad was probably stashing his tools in the shed at that very moment and starting to worry about whether I'd make it back before the downpour.

"We'll be back tomorrow, okay?" I said to the cats as I reached under the plastic bags and carefully placed a handful of kibble inside the box. Meanwhile, Bradley folded up the top of the food bag and put it under the bench, where hopefully it would stay dry.

We were about halfway home when the skies really opened up. There was a rumbling of thunder, followed by a crack of lightning—a little too close together for comfort. But even though we tried, we couldn't run any faster. Our flip-flops kept sliding off in the puddles.

Bradley and I went our separate ways at the corner. I could see my dad waiting for me on the porch with a big towel. He didn't look worried, though. At least, not until he caught sight of my leg.

"Clara!" he said. "Are you bleeding?"

Mixed with the rainwater that was running down my leg, it really did look like a lot of blood. "It's okay," I lied. "Last week's scab just fell off."

After I'd cleaned the cut and put on some Band-Aids, I sat down on the couch near the window. Usually, I loved the cozy feeling of being inside during a storm and the *plink-plink* sound of rain hitting the porch roof. But that afternoon, the downpour felt relentless. All I could think about was Isadorabella and her kittens in that flimsy box.

"Everything okay, kiddo?" Dad asked on his way through to the TV room. I wanted to tell him. But as much as I hated the idea of Izzy-B and the kittens out in the rain, I hated the idea of them trapped in cages at Animal Services even more.

"Yup." I plastered on a smile, and then grabbed my sketchbook and opened it to a fresh page to distract myself. I spent the next hour trying to think up ideas for my next Claymation film, @*Cat: The Movie—The Sequel*, but every storyline I came up with felt like it had already been done, and my mind kept drifting back to the churchyard.

CONCEPT 1:
Robo-Cat

A crime-fighting robot cat defends the streets of Animalea.

CONCEPT 2:
Cod-Zilla

A giant Plasticine fish has emerged from the ocean and is on the loose in Animalea. Can @Cat save the day?

CONCEPT 3:
Furry Potter and the Odor of the Phoenix

A young and furry computerized cat learns of her true identity as a wizard. Now she must use her magic (and her advanced sense of smell) to hunt down the elusive phoenix.

It rained all afternoon and well into the evening, but the next morning I could tell, before I'd even opened my eyes, that the sun was out. The rhythmic banging coming from the backyard was a dead giveaway: Dad was back at work on his deck.

I threw on a T-shirt and a pair of shorts and went out to see him without even stopping in the kitchen for breakfast. (And everyone knows it's the most important meal of the day.)

"There she is." Dad shielded his eyes from the sun. "Would you mind holding these planks in place for me while I screw them down?"

Because the old deck had already been ripped off the back of the house and the new one was nothing but a few wooden beams that would eventually support the floor, there was a huge drop-off outside the patio doors. I took a flying leap and landed in the grass with ninja-like grace.

"No problemo, Dad!"

"You're in a good mood today," he noted as he lined a plank of wood up with the house, letting it rest on the beams.

I held the board tightly while he drilled it into

place. And when he stood back to look at our work with a satisfied smile, I could tell he was in a good mood too. I seized the opportunity.

"You know, I was thinking ..." I started. "You and Mom said no to getting a cat, and I completely understand." Dad gave me a dubious look. He must have known there was a "but" coming. "But," I went on, "have you considered how great it would be to get a kitten?

"If you get a kitten," I explained, before he could object, "you get to be an influence in its life right from the start. You can train it to do all kinds of amazing things."

"Really?" Dad raised his eyebrows in a way that suggested he didn't believe me but wouldn't mind being convinced. If there was one thing my dad liked, it was amazing things. And between him and my mom, he was definitely the bigger pushover. If I could get him on my side, he just might be able to influence her.

"Really," I answered. We lined up the next board. "If you use positive reinforcements, like treats, and you start when they're young, you can teach a kitten to come when you call."

My dad didn't look amazed yet, so I pulled out something more incredible. "You can even teach it how to use the toilet instead of a litter box." I'd watched a video about it online. The cat, an orange tabby named Rupert, even flushed.

"I don't know, Clara," Dad said. "Getting a new pet is a big decision. It's something we'd all need to agree on as a family."

I nodded somberly, but inside my head, I was doing the happy dance.

What I looked like on the outside.

"Those are wise words, Father. I completely agree."

What I was feeling on the inside.

"Eeeeeeeee! We're getting a kitten!!!"

After all, my dad had just said "I don't know." That was a HUGE step up from no. In fact, it was halfway to yes!

I felt certain that, if I just kept at it, I could convince my parents to let me keep at least a few of Izzy-B's kittens.

"I already cleaned Bijou's cage last night, and I put away my clean laundry," I told my dad. "Is it okay if I go to the park with Bradley?"

"Sure," he said. "Could you help me with just a few more boards first, though?"

And because keeping my dad in a good mood was of the utmost importance for my kitten-adoption plan, I was glad to help out. Anyway, it was satisfying to see the boards lining up one after another. I really did have a knack for construction—which got me thinking: If my future career as a stop-motion moviemaker didn't pan out, I could always become a master deck builder. I wouldn't stop at your average, run-of-the-mill decks, though ...

Behold! The patented, trademarked Clara Humble Quadruple-Decker Deck!

And that gave me another idea ...

At first, I wasn't sure how I was going to pull it off, but then fate stepped in.

"Pee break!" Dad announced. "Thanks, Clara. I'll take it from here when I get back." He took off his tool belt and headed inside.

I waited until he'd closed the screen door behind him, and then I very quietly borrowed a few odds and ends I was pretty sure my dad wouldn't need anyway. I loaded them into the wobbly wheeled, cobwebby red wagon that had been sitting in our yard for years and set off. Bradley and I had kitten caretaking to do.

The Caboodle

The Caboodle: Was it yet another of my unquestionably clever plans, or was it cursed from the start? It's hard to say ... but one thing is certain: It was the beginning of the end of our friendship as we knew it.

"What is a caboodle, exactly?" Bradley asked that first morning.

After we'd arrived at the churchyard, it had taken us a minute or two to pry the chain-link fence up enough to fit the wagonload of stuff through—and now we were struggling to pull our cart of supplies in the tall weeds.

A caboodle? Truthfully, I wasn't 100 percent sure. It was something I'd heard Momo say once. "I'll take the whole kitten caboodle," she'd proclaimed at a garage sale, buying a never-used litter box, a water dish, and a bunch of toys for Wiggles and Fatty-Fatty-Two-Tip, her big old tomcats.

"'Caboodle' means all the things kittens and cats need," I told Bradley matter-of-factly as I dug my heels into the ground and tugged on the wagon handle. "And what they need now is a safe, warm, weatherproof shelter."

"Oh no," Bradley said as we rounded the church. I followed his gaze. "And a place to keep the food."

I abandoned the wagon and walked over to pick up a scrap of bright-orange packaging. It was part of our bag of Opti-1 Feline Nutrition Formula. There was kibble spilled out on the ground all over the place, and it had gone to mush in the rain.

I gathered the remaining pieces of the ripped bag. "I guess raccoons like cat food," I said with a sigh. "We'll need to buy more today."

"Yeah," Bradley said. "It's your turn to pay, though, right?"

"Actually ..." I started. I was still weeks away from paying back the advance I'd taken on my allowance—which was a mere five dollars a week. Bradley, on the other hand, got ten dollars. Plus, his grandma gave him and his sister twenty-dollar bills whenever they visited—and he'd just been there two weeks before. "Since I brought all the stuff for building the cat shelter, it might be fair if you paid for the food."

The old Bradley probably wouldn't have made such a big deal about it. And he was still the most generous person I knew—but I kept forgetting that these days, my best friend wasn't quite so willing to do things my way all the time.

"That's not fair at all!" he said. "You got this stuff for free from your backyard."

"Well, yeah," I answered. "But I'm also the one who knows how to put it all together. So that's worth something. Plus," I went on when I could see that he wasn't buying my argument, "I don't have any money right now. And we can't just let Izzy-B starve." I gave Bradley a pleading look and, thankfully, at the sound of our voices, the mother cat emerged from her box to do the rest.

Mew. She looked up at us adorably with big, hungry eyes. *Mew.*

"I'm trying to save up for headphones for my metal detector." Bradley frowned. "But fine. Stay right here and start building something to store food in. I'll go to Andy's. But you have to pay me back for half later."

"I will," I promised. "I definitely will."

Bradley started off through the weeds. "Oh, and also," I called behind him, "could you get some candy?"

He turned and raised his eyebrows.

"Not for me! For Shane! Remember? We need to keep him quiet, or else he'll tell our parents about the cats."

"Fine," Bradley muttered. "But just so you know, I'm getting the cheaper cat food this time."

I opened my mouth to argue—after all, Izzy was nursing six kittens. If there was ever a time when she needed the absolute finest in feline nutrition, this was it—but then I shut it again. I didn't want to push Bradley too far.

All the same, there were certain things I just wasn't willing to compromise on. As the kittens grew, so did the Caboodle—and I was determined not to settle for anything less than top-of-the-line all the way.

Day 1 of construction was all about the food box. That alone took most of the wood I'd brought, but I was proud of the finished product. It was solid, with a lid that tied shut in four different places, using strong bits of rope we'd found in the grass. One hundred percent rain- and raccoon-proof!

On day 2, I brought more supplies, and it was on to the Caboodle. It started with a wooden rectangular structure to replace the flimsy cardboard box. The scraps I'd borrowed from my dad had already been cut to a good size, so it wasn't too hard to nail them together, leaving an opening at one end. Bradley didn't have as much construction experience as I did, but he helped to carry things and held the boards in place while I nailed them. All in all—including sanding the outside and decorating and painting the inside—it took us four days.

Caboodle Construction:
DAY 5

Bedroom of Caboodle is done. Kittens can rest easy!

Kitten Development:
DAY 6

Ocean-blue eyes begin to open. Caution: Do not look directly into kitten eyes. Your heart will melt.

After the main Caboodle was finished, Bradley stood back and dusted off his hands. "Looks great!" he said with a satisfied smile.

And it was definitely adequate ... but great?! I'd seen an article in the newspaper not too long before about kids reading books to animals in pet shelters. I couldn't remember much about it except that it was supposed to be a good thing. Probably because it boosted their brain development. The cats needed a library. There was no doubt in my mind.

By the time we finished the library, the kittens were nine days old. Their once-flattened ears perked up and they tilted their cute little heads. "It's like they're listening to every word!" Bradley said incredulously, flipping the pages of a book.

I nodded knowingly and then went to get some more scraps of wood from the wagon.

"What are you doing now?" Bradley asked.

As Bradley had been reading *The Cat in the Hat*, I'd noticed that Twinkle Nose, one of the biggest kittens, had been inching forward—just a little. According to *Felines for Fools*, kittens started to walk between two and three weeks. That was mere days away!

At first, Bradley was iffy about the idea of the deluxe kitten jungle gym ... but I'm pretty sure he saw the wisdom of my ways. At fifteen days old, Prickle, Pickle, and Peary were making their way up the balance beam with stuttery steps, and Rosie, Bouncer, and Twinkle Nose were already checking out the tunnel slide we'd made from an old piece of bendy tubing I'd found in my garage.

Caboodle Construction:
DAY 14

Kitten Development:
DAY 15

Jungle gym added! The Caboodle grows more awesome by the minute.

Kittens are walking in such a wobbly way. OMG! Awwwwww!

"Look!" he said, laughing. "Rosie's piloting the kitten-copter!" The gray-and-white kitten was perched in the pretend helicopter I'd attached to the very top of the jungle gym. I'd made the propeller out of old popsicle sticks and the steering wheel from a yogurt lid.

Bradley finished sanding one last rough spot on the balance beam and then stepped back.

"They're playing hard," I said with a sigh. "They'll need a place to rest."

"Like their bedroom?" Bradley asked.

"I was thinking more like an outdoor living area. You know, for lounging?"

"They lounge pretty much everywhere." He pointed to Izzy-B, who was flopped over in a patch of dirt, sunning her belly while her babies played.

But Bradley was missing the point! Tips on how to build a backyard oasis were in all my mom's decorating magazines. And if the rich and famous had stylish outdoor living spaces, shouldn't Izzy-B and her kittens have one too? Bradley hadn't seemed so sure—although, in the end, he'd agreed. He'd even made some cool kitten-sized hammock chairs out of old T-shirts and twigs the next afternoon.

It wasn't until the very last day of July that Bradley really lost his patience.

I was working on the formal dining room (the

next logical addition to the Caboodle) and had just finished installing a crystal chandelier made from one of my mom's old earrings. It was catching the light beautifully and would set the tone for many elegant meals of kibble to come. But instead of admiring its sparkle, my best friend was sulking.

That morning, he'd brought an old beach towel from home for the cats to curl up on—and I guess I'd hurt his feelings. The towel was a nice idea, but it had holes in it, and I just so happened to have found my old Hello Kitty bedsheet in a box of stuff destined for donation that same morning. It was going to go perfectly with the color scheme of the bedroom—pink and purple.

"Fine," Bradley had said in a grumpy voice. "Whatever you think is best."

And then he'd taken his old towel over by the church and sat down on it. But even though he was mad at me, it turned out to be a lucky thing. Because if Bradley had been busy working instead of moping around that morning, he might not have heard the yelling ...

"Noooooo! I said I want the princess bucket!" It was the very loud voice of a little kid, and it was coming from the sidewalk. I didn't recognize it right away, but Bradley did. Probably because he'd heard it every single day for the last five years.

"That's Val!" he whispered urgently, already getting up off the ground. I stopped spinning the chandelier. If Bradley's little sister was out on the sidewalk, that could only mean one thing ...

Bradley motioned with his head. We crawled through the weeds as silently as we could manage until we were close enough to overhear but could still stay safely hidden.

"Listen to my words," came Svetlana's measured voice from the other side of the fence. "We have the blue bucket. We are not going home for the princess bucket." At that, Val started to wail even louder.

"I'm counting to three. If you don't stop that behavior, we will go home. And you will not get to play with Bradley and Clara at the park. One ..." Svetlana began.

I breathed a sigh of relief, and Bradley seemed to relax as well. On a scale of 1 to 10 for stubbornness, Bradley's sister was an 11.5. And anyone who knew Svetlana knew she didn't mess around. She'd stay true to her word—even though it was going to mean carrying a kicking, screaming five-year-old all the way home.

"Two ..." Svetlana counted as the screaming continued. "And ..." she said, not even bothering to stretch out the word to give Val extra time. There was an almost instant silence. Bradley and I looked at each other in terror.

"Good choice," Svetlana said. "Let's go."

"Holy cheese," Bradley whispered. "We are so dead."

"No we're not," I whispered back. "I know a way."

I crawled to the fence and stuck my head out. Svetlana and Val were halfway up the block. We'd be busted if either one of them looked back, but if we didn't go right away, we'd never make it in time.

"Come on!" We looked both ways and then dashed across the street. "Run!" I said. "Faster than you've ever run before!" To make it to the park before Val and Svetlana, we'd need to circle the block, jump the fence, and cross the soccer field— all before they made it down Peter Street and crossed at the lights.

Luckily, Bradley and I had both been on the track team the year before. We were in top physical form. And even more fortunately, as we skidded off the park path into the sandpit, we saw Svetlana's friend Sarah. She and Svetlana were standing across the street at the lights, probably talking about the latest scandal on *The Rich and the Restless* (Svetlana and Sarah's favorite soap opera), while Val tugged impatiently on Svetlana's hand.

"We're safe," I said with a smile. But instead of thanking me for my quick thinking, Bradley exhaled heavily.

"This has to stop." He shook his head seriously. "We can't keep sneaking around."

"Don't worry," I said. "It's just until my parents say I can adopt some kittens, and that's definitely going to be any day now."

So, yes. It had been taking a little longer than I would have liked, but my mom and dad were definitely warming up to the idea. I'd casually left some pictures of kittens on the dining room table that morning, and I'd noticed my mom admiring them while she drank her coffee. Plus, while staining the deck, my dad had used a grocery store flyer to set his wet brush on. It had been open to a page advertising a special on unscented litter. Coincidence? Maybe not.

"Even if your mom and dad do say yes to one kitten," Bradley said, "what about Spike and the other five? We'll still need to find them homes. And my mom said not to ask her again because her answer's a firm no."

I glanced across the street. Svetlana had finished her conversation—or else she'd finally gotten sick of listening to Val whine. Either way, they were crossing the road and Val was waving to us.

"You're right," I began. I knew from experience that starting off by agreeing with Bradley helped him see things my way. "There's no way my parents will ever say yes to seven cats in the house. But I've been thinking ... what if the cats didn't live in my house?"

I motioned toward a playhouse on the other side of the jungle gym. "What if instead they lived in their own house? About that size. Only in my backyard. It's obvious that we're great at building stuff. We could easily make them a year-round shelter. We could even heat it for the winter ...

and it won't cost that much, since my dad gets a discount at the hardware store."

"I don't know, Clara." Bradley wrinkled his nose. "I doubt your parents would agree to that."

"Of course they will!" I said. "I mean, sure, they're not cat people yet ... but that's only because they haven't met Peary."

Peary, the smallest of the kittens—who I'd named based on the fact that his bum looked almost exactly like an upside-down pear—was a true charmer.

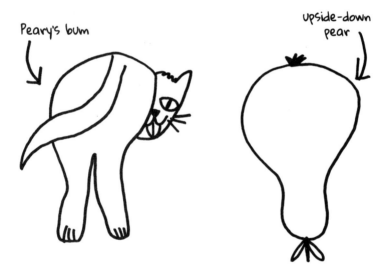

Peary's bum

upside-down pear

He had the cutest way of cocking his head to one side, and he liked to ride on my shoulders and fall asleep with his body draped around my neck, purring the whole time, like an especially adorable vibrating scarf. I'd already decided that he was the one I most wanted to adopt ... and once my mom and dad fell in love with him like I had, there was no way they'd be heartless enough to separate him from his whole family.

"They'll definitely say yes," I reassured Bradley. "I know they will!"

"But when?" Bradley asked. "Look," he went on when I didn't have an answer to that question, "I just think we should be doing something. I mean, besides making them chandeliers," he scoffed.

"I think ..." Bradley paused, and then he stood up and walked around the jungle gym's fire pole in a slow circle, "I think it's time we considered telling an adult."

"No way!" I shouted. Then I got ahold of myself and lowered my voice. Svetlana was sitting down on the bench on the other side of the jungle gym. She was busy putting sunscreen on Val.

"I mean ... not yet." Because I knew how Bradley's mind worked, I pulled out a fact. "You read it yourself in *Felines for Fools*: Kittens should stay with their mothers until they're at least eight weeks old. And they're only about three weeks old now! If we tell a grown-up, they'll get sent to Animal Services. And if that happens, they could get separated from Izzy-B."

Bradley considered this information, but it still didn't seem to change his mind. "That might be true," he said, "but look what almost just happened ... again!" He motioned with his head toward Svetlana. "And since I'm the one who's ten ... if we get caught sneaking around, I'm the one who's going to be responsible."

I was getting pretty tired of hearing about how much older and more mature Bradley thought he was ... and I was on the verge of telling him so—but something stopped me. The truth was, I needed him on my side. Plus, he kind of had a point. This had been our closest call yet, but it hadn't been our only near miss.

Two weeks earlier—on a really hot day—my dad had come to check on us and bring us some cold water. Luckily, we'd actually been at the park when he arrived, filling up the cat's water dish at the drinking fountain. And another time, my mom had driven by the park on her lunch break and said at dinner that she hadn't seen us there. Thankfully, I'd managed to convince her we must have just been in the wooded area at the back, looking for treasure.

"Even if we don't get caught," Bradley went on, "we're going to run out of kibble soon. I'm paying for everything. And I'm almost out of money! Plus, according to *Felines for Fools*, in two more weeks, the kittens will need to start eating special kitten food. How am I supposed to pay for that too? And then there's Shane," he added with a sigh.

He had a point. Bribing Shane to keep quiet about the kittens had been costing Bradley a small fortune—and with each passing day, Shane seemed to demand more in exchange for his silence. The day before, Bradley had bought every last gummy worm from Andy's store.

"I'll figure it out, okay?" I pleaded. "I'll find a way to pay you back for my half of the cat food. I'll even pay for the special kitten food myself— and I'll keep Shane quiet. You don't have to worry about anything. All you need to do is not tell. Just for a little while longer!" I made my biggest, saddest eyes at him. "Please!" I added in my sweetest voice.

Bradley sighed, which I took as a yes. "Two more weeks," he said. "Tops. If you aren't allowed to adopt them by then, we definitely need to ask an adult for help."

"Okay, fine," I said. "Two weeks."

It was plenty of time to convince my parents to say yes to Peary and a bigger, even-better backyard Caboodle and—in the meantime—to raise the money I'd need for cat food and bribing Shane. The only problem was, I had no idea how I was going to do any of those things.

@Cat: The Movie— The Sequel

When I got home for dinner, I found my parents out in the yard. The top tier of the deck was completely finished, and sitting right in the middle, in all its shining glory, was the GrillMaster Legend Four-Burner Gas BBQ with JetFire Ignition.

It was bigger than I'd thought it would be, and more high-tech. Between the two huge side trays (that looked like wings), its enormous cooking hatch, and the zillions of knobs and dials, I half-expected it to blast off into space.

"Ain't she a beaut?" Dad said with a cowboy accent. "Watch this." He pressed a button on the front and the BBQ blazed to life. "Four burners with a single touch!" Dad grinned like a kid. He used one of the knobs to lower the flames to just the right level and then took a plate from my mom.

It had three steaks on it, slathered in his special smoky, sweet 'n' spicy sauce. Dad placed them each gently on the grill and added an extra squirt of sauce from a bottle he had tucked in his apron pocket.

"Oh. Like it?" Dad said when he noticed me looking. "Chuck at the hardware store threw it in when I picked up the grill."

I smiled because, at first, I did like the apron. The cow looked funny in her sunglasses. But a second later, as the smell of the sizzling steak wafted through the air, it hit me: The cartoon cow was cooking a steak. Steak was made of cow! That cow was cheerfully cooking her aunt or uncle ... maybe even one of her own baby calves!

"Clara? What's wrong?" Mom asked. She'd returned the plate to the kitchen and walked back out the sliding doors just in time to see me go pale.

"I don't want steak tonight." I sat down on the

edge of the deck and let my feet dangle over the side.

"You feeling okay?" Mom rubbed my back and then pressed a cool hand to my forehead.

"No. I mean, yes. I just definitely want to be a vegetarian."

"Clara," Mom said. "We've talked about this ..."

Ever since our class had gone on a field trip to Brownberry Farms the year before and my friend Abby had decided to become vegetarian, I'd been thinking it over.

It somehow felt wrong to eat a juicy hamburger after you'd fed Daisy the Dairy Cow handfuls of grass and gazed into her soulful brown eyes. Since that day, I'd definitely wanted to give up meat ... but there was one problem: vegetables. I hated them.

"You ate half a pound of bacon last weekend, made an oinking noise, and asked for more," Dad pointed out.

And obviously, bacon. I loved bacon.

"And you know," Mom reminded me in her this-is-serious voice, "being vegetarian means eating lots of legumes, like lentils and chickpeas. Fresh veggies too. Arugula, kale, parsnips ..."

Just like the last time we'd had this conversation, she was purposely naming all the grossest vegetables so I'd think long and hard about my decision. But I didn't need to think long and hard anymore. Now that I was the caretaker of six helpless kittens and their mother, my already incredible love for animals had reached a new height. And if I was truly a friend to ALL animals (and I was!), how could I care for a chinchilla, one cat, and six kittens while slathering sauce on a cow?

"Do we have any kale?" I asked in a shaky voice.

Luckily, we didn't. My parents agreed to let me try eating vegetarian for a few weeks, and then we'd re-evaluate. But first I had to promise to eat a balanced diet with lots of meat-free protein. That night, I made myself a peanut butter and banana sandwich for dinner while my mom and dad split the third steak.

And afterward, while my parents were waiting for the news to come on, I took the opportunity to make some headway in my "convince them to get a kitten" plan. Only this time, I didn't waste time talking.

"Want to see something adorable?" I carried the laptop over to my parents, sat down between them on the couch, and pressed Play on the squeal-worthy video I had loaded up. I was planning to let the magical cuteness of kittens do the work for me ... except instead of three kittens playing in a box of Styrofoam packing peanuts, this came on:

My mom actually LOLed out loud. "Is that a real product?" she asked.

"It is. We have them down at the hardware store," Dad answered. "They're selling like hotcakes too. Probably as gag gifts, but still ..."

"Well, they are *egg-stra-ordinary,*" Mom said with a wink.

By now, the video of the cute kittens had come on, but my parents were so busy talking about square eggs that they barely noticed.

"If you can sell an egg cuber, you can sell anything," Mom said. "Those internet ads must work."

Dad nodded. "I bet some of them generate a good profit for the video-makers too."

At the word "profit," my ears perked up. "What do you mean?" I asked.

"Mean about what?" Dad said. Finally, the video was working its magic. He was busy watching a kitten try to climb out of a box and then fall back in. "Oh, ad profits?" he asked, taking a guess before I could answer. "Well, every time someone watches one of those internet ads, the advertiser pays the video's creator a bit of money. If enough people watch, it can really add up."

Suddenly, I was also interested in square eggs. "Add up to how much?"

"I guess it varies," Dad answered. "A few hundred a month, maybe ... or in some cases, maybe thousands."

Thousands?! Just for posting a video on the

internet?! I watched one of the kittens disappear beneath the Styrofoam and then pop back up, startling itself with the noise it had made. I mean, sure, these kittens were cute—but they weren't as cute as our kittens. Plus, the video we were watching didn't even have a plot.

And that was when my big idea came to me. All I needed to do to raise money for the cat family was make a video—and I knew I could produce one a hundred times better than most of the stuff online.

After all, the @Cat film I'd made at camp had been a huge success. And, sure, I hadn't had much luck thinking of a story for a sequel—but suddenly I could see the problem as plain as day. It wasn't me, it was the method I'd been planning to use!

Claymation was slow and tedious work. It was all wrong for a movie about a character as dynamic as @Cat. What I needed to make a blockbuster film were live actors—or "cat-ors," to be exact. And, luckily, I knew seven of the cutest felines in Gleason who were just right for the job.

"Scene one, take fourteen." I scissored my arms like one of those clipboard things they use in the moviemaking biz. "And three, two, one, action!"

It was mid-morning the next day, and for the fourteenth time, I'd managed to sneak up behind Izzy-B and put on her @Cat antenna (a pipe cleaner with a pom-pom hot-glued to the end). I'd also made her a cape from part of an old red T-shirt. She looked great, or she would have if she'd kept the costume on. For scene one, all I needed her to do was sit, gazing out over the jungles of Animalea (actually the weedy churchyard) but, like many stars, Izzy had her own vision.

She swatted the antenna off with her front paw. Again. "Cut," I said with a sigh.

Shane Biggs switched off his cell phone and threw his hands up in the air. "Seriously?!" he yelled.

And, yes, I know you might be thinking that exact same thing: Seriously?! Shane Biggs?! What was he doing on the set of my blockbuster internet cat film? Trust me—I'd asked myself the same question, but the unfortunate answer I kept coming back to was this: I needed him.

For one thing, Bradley was at JTT with Nelson that week, so he wouldn't be around to help. But, even more inconveniently, it meant I needed to ask to go play at the "park" (aka the churchyard) alone—and even though I was going to be ten in a mere 30.5 days, my parents were being so stubborn.

"You know the rule. Dad and I only feel comfortable if you're with a friend. Find someone we know who's at least ten," my mom had said that morning at breakfast when I'd pleaded my case. But there weren't any other ten-year-olds on our block—not unless you counted Shane.

What's more, my lack of a ten-year-old friend wasn't the only problem. Even though I could handle being the scriptwriter, director, producer, head of props, costume consultant, location scout, stunt trainer, and casting coordinator, I didn't have a camera to film the movie with—and I only knew one kid with access to an almost unlimited amount of technology, including his very own cell phone with a 50-megapixel camera.

"Oh, quit whining," I told Shane as I picked the antenna up off the ground and tiptoed toward

Izzy-B again. He definitely had the easy job. I'd already been scratched twice by our star.

Plus, I was going to make this whole thing worth his while. For filming the movie as well as his continued silence about the cat family, I'd offered him 30 percent of all future earnings (then I'd reluctantly agreed when he'd talked me up to 50). Still, I figured I'd have lots left over to pay for cat food and supplies for the backyard Caboodle I had planned.

Of course, first we had to make the movie ...

"Look," I said. "Let's just skip to scene two, okay? The one where @Cat discovers the sickly stray kittens in the garbage heap."

As it turned out, Peary was a natural on camera. Shane and I got back to work, and my favorite kitten brought a tear to my eye when, as a young stray meeting @Cat for the first time, he rubbed his face lovingly against her leg. In fact, pretty much all of the kittens were Hollywood-worthy that morning.

We breezed through scenes three and four— where the kittens went back to @Cat's secret training facility to be nursed back to health.

@Cat fed the kittens to fortify them. But, oh no! What's this? She accidentally gave them superfood! Almost immediately, strange things began to happen.

And we probably would have made it all the way through the first page of my storyboard if Shane's cell phone hadn't started ringing.

"What?" Shane barked into his phone. He paused. "Yeah, yeah. Okay, fine," he said through gritted teeth. He hung up. "My mom says I need to come home for lunch."

I glanced down at my digital precision wristwatch and was surprised to see that it was nearly noon.

"I'm supposed to tell you you're invited," he went on, making a face. "My mom already called your dad. We're having grilled cheese and banana bread."

I considered that information. My dad had taken the week off work. He was supposed to be looking after me—but I didn't need much looking after. Mostly, he was working on the second tier of the deck. At my house, lunch would be the Value Brand veggie burgers my dad had picked up at the store that morning. And Shane's mom did bake the best banana bread. "Okay," I said. Shane rolled his eyes in excitement and we started to pack up our gear.

All the same, ten minutes later, when Janet met us at the door with glasses of ice-cold lemonade, I knew I'd made the right call.

"Wow," she said as she watched us gulp it down, "you must have been playing hard at the park." She was grinning, no doubt at the thought of all the fresh air Shane had inhaled that morning.

I looked around their house like I always do when I go there, thinking of Momo and remembering where all her stuff used to be.

"Why don't you go wash up for lunch first, Shane?" Janet suggested. "Then Clara can have a turn."

Shane grumbled, but he kicked off his sandals and headed down the hall. Meanwhile, I followed the smell of banana bread into the kitchen. The loaf was perfectly golden. I could tell at a glance that it even had chocolate chips.

"So?" Janet pulled out a stool for me at the kitchen island. "Did you guys have fun?" But she didn't even wait for me to answer. "Thanks for including Shane, Clara." She smiled warmly as she reached for a knife and started to slice the loaf. It let out a waft of banana-chocolate-scented steam. "I know it means a lot to him. He still misses his friends back in California. Moving is so hard on a kid."

Her eyes were getting misty as she talked. "Anyway, I'm glad that we bought a house on the same block as you and Bradley. You're both such nice kids."

I looked down at my fingernails so Janet wouldn't see the truth in my eyes. I mean, basically, in a lot of ways I was a pretty nice kid … but not nice enough to hang out with Shane by choice.

"After lunch, I'll show you what I'm working on, if you want." Janet changed the subject as Shane walked into the kitchen. "I'm doing some drawings for a kids' magazine—all about cats. They're not as funny as @Cat, of course." She smiled.

"Okay," I said, my mouth already full of the grilled cheese sandwich Janet had set down in front of me. (Technically, I was supposed to have washed my hands first. If Momo had been there, she would have said I had enough dirt under my fingernails to grow tomatoes in. But thankfully Janet didn't seem to notice.)

After she'd cleared the plates, Janet took me to her study. Her drawings were adorable—especially the one of a cat stealing a sock from a laundry basket. Janet told me how, when she was little, she had a cat named Moth who used to do the same thing.

Then we got busy talking about @Cat, and even though I couldn't tell her about the movie we were filming without spilling the beans about the secret cat family, I showed her one of the sketches I was working on for the movie poster, and she gave me tips on drawing the flying kittens to make them look even more 3-D.

Finally, Janet had to get back to work, so I went to find Shane—which wasn't hard to do. I just followed the sounds of his video-game music. He was in his room (Momo's old spare room), hunched over in front of his laptop. I stopped in the doorway near a big *Legend of Zelda* poster. I half-expected Shane to tell me his room was a no-girls-allowed zone or something—but he waved me in.

"Come see," he said, not taking his eyes off the screen.

I tiptoed around some dirty socks, came to stand behind him, and did a double take. Instead of the shoot-'em-up video game I'd expected on the screen, Shane had some video-editing software open. It wasn't the same program I'd used at Claymation Kids, but I recognized some of the features, like audio equalizer (which I'd used to make Poodle Noodle's voice sound just the right amount of evil) and color correction (for adjusting the hue and saturation until @Cat's red cape stood out like a beacon of hope).

Shane hit Play on one of the windows and music started. It had a low, steady beat. Suddenly, an image flashed across the screen: a circle with the outline of a building in it. I recognized it just from the shape of the steeple. Shane had designed a logo with the abandoned church on it!

"From Churchyard Entertainment." Suddenly, the background crackled, as if it had just been hit by lightning, and the text changed "... In association with @Cat Productions."

The lightning effect happened again and then the screen kind of split, so that one side had a picture, and the other side was black with white comic-book-style writing on it.

"Her name is not Flea Bags," I said, giving Shane a shove on the shoulder, but truthfully, it was a minor detail considering how awesome the rest of the movie intro was.

A bunch of cool electric guitars came in and the drumbeat got louder. Then the split screen shifted so the text was on the other side. Peary leaped into the frame. He was probably chasing a fly in real life, but the way Shane had captured it and then slowed it down, it really looked like he was flying. "And featuring Peary in the role of Super-Kitten #1 ..."

After that, the video stopped. "I'm going to add the other kittens next," Shane said with a shrug.

"Not bad," I said, nodding. I didn't want it to go to his head, so I didn't tell him what I was actually thinking. (That it was off-the-charts awesome!) In fact, it was beyond even my wildest dreams for how good our movie might turn out, and I'd had some pretty wild dreams.

I want to start by thanking all the little people and small cats who made this possible...

In fact, it was going to take the internet by storm! I sat down on Shane's unmade bed and gazed out the window as I imagined how great it would be. Forget thousands of dollars in ad revenue. We might be looking at millions! With money like that, I could build a backyard shelter big enough to house every stray cat in the city of Gleason. And why stop there? If this thing got as big as I thought it might, I could help ALL animals in need: from caterpillars to cattle!

I leaned forward so I could see what Shane was doing. "Once we're done the opening credits," I said, "you're going to put in the title, right? It needs to say *@Cat and the Unstoppable 6*. And can you do that lightning thing behind it again? Only faster and a little brighter?"

Shane nodded and selected a pull-down menu. And just like that, we were on our way to internet fame.

The Walking Stairs

When you love animals the way I do, sometimes you need to make some tough calls to protect them—some really tough calls.

That night, while my parents enjoyed lamb shish kebabs, I had the Value Brand veggie burgers I'd avoided at lunch. (I'd had some pretty good veggie burgers at Abby's house before, but these ones tasted like warmed-up sponges.)

"Well?" Dad asked from across the table. "How are they?"

Instead of answering, I washed down a mouthful with milk before taking another bite. If eating sponge-burgers was what it took to save animals, I'd do it all day long.

"I think she loves it," Mom said with just a hint of a smile. I couldn't tell if she was teasing or not, and I was glad at first when my parents moved on to another subject. It was bad enough having to eat those things. Being teased about it was next-level cruel.

"The second tier of the deck is really coming along." Mom nodded toward the work Dad had done that afternoon while I'd secretly headed back to the churchyard to film with Shane. "How long till it's finished?"

CRUEL-OMETER

OFF THE CHARTS:
Being teased about eating sponge-burgers

30 DEGREES:
Actually having to eat sponge-burgers

20 DEGREES:
Being denied a kitten

10 DEGREES:
When your parents make you go to bed and then they watch movies with bad words and eat secret snacks

SLIGHTLY ABOVE 0:
Dentist appointments on weekends

"Well ..." Dad began. He took a juicy-looking bite of kebab and chewed thoughtfully. "I thought I'd be done this weekend, but ... it's the weirdest thing. I can't find the stairs."

"The stairs?" Mom asked.

"Well, the pieces of wood for the stairs. I had them precut and ready to go weeks ago, but they've vanished."

"Stairs don't just get up and walk away," Mom

said reasonably.

Dad shrugged. "These ones did."

I stared at my plate. Obviously, those pieces of wood that I'd assumed were scraps were stairs. Only these days, they were a luxury kitty condominium that doubled as @Cat's secret lair and state-of-the-art super-cat training facility. It was a more creative use of the materials, if you asked me—but that didn't stop me from feeling bad about taking them.

"Anyway," Dad went on. "I'll need to buy more wood. I've misplaced a few tools too. Like my medium-sized hammer and the good Phillips-head screwdriver."

Mom grimaced. How much the deck was costing—even with my dad's employee discount—had come up more than a few times recently, and so had my dad's habit of losing his stuff. Before they could start arguing, I changed the topic.

"Can I go to the park with Bradley and Shane after dinner?" I asked.

"Shane's coming with you?" Mom asked with slightly raised eyebrows. Ever since he'd moved in next door, my mom had been asking me to include

Shane in our games, which I'd mostly flat-out refused to do, for obvious reasons.

"Clara and Shane played together all day," Dad announced proudly, as if he'd personally managed to make us be friends.

"Well, I think that's great." Mom took another bite of lamb kebab and I watched her chew with envy (I bet it tasted amazing!) and outrage (Baby sheep! On a stick!). "Of course you can go to the park with your friends. Just be home by seven," she added.

As soon as I'd choked down the last of my dinner, I went next door to get Shane, and then we cut through my yard to Bradley's. We found him on his back patio playing with a super-bouncy ball—and if he was surprised to see Shane with me, he didn't let it show on his face.

"Oh, hi guys," he said. "Catch!" He lobbed the ball at the pavement. It went as high as the fence. I stuck out my hand and grabbed it easily, even though it was barely bigger than a marble. (Not to brag, but I'm a bit of a super-bouncy-ball expert. You can tell by the number of balls stuck on the flat roof at the back of my house, which is an impressive two stories tall.)

"Cool!" I said as I examined it. The ball had a swirly rainbow look, but it was also kind of clear with sparkles. I'd never seen one quite like it. I gave it a good bounce and managed to get it nearly as high as Bradley's garage on the first try.

"I know, right?" Bradley said proudly. "Today at JTT, we did geocaching. It's like a digital treasure hunt using GPS. Me and Nelson found this cache no one else could—deep in a marshy area—and he let me keep the treasure inside, which was this ball."

I looked down at the ball I'd just caught. Suddenly, I didn't like it quite as much.

"That's nice," I said, bouncing it back to Bradley. I led the way down the narrow path at the side of his house. "We had a good day too. Actually, Shane's helping me with an exciting project."

I assumed he'd be intrigued. So I was surprised when, instead of asking what our project was, he went straight back to his new favorite subjects: know-it-all Nelson and totally tedious treasure tracking.

"Tomorrow we're taking our metal detectors to the beach and having a picnic." He bounced the ball every few steps. "Nelson says you wouldn't believe the stuff people lose at the beach. One time, he found a cheese grater in the sand. Isn't that weird? I mean, who grates cheese at the beach?"

I had no idea what people did with cheese at the beach—and I didn't especially care. I just knew that if I heard one more word about Nelson or JTT, I would scream.

I shrugged in answer to his cheese question and changed the subject. "Anyway. It's pretty exciting. We're making @*Cat: The Movie—The Sequel* using the cats as live actors. And you should see the intro Shane edited together today. It's better than some Hollywood films."

Shane, who was walking beside me, smirked a little at the praise.

"We're going to post it online when it's done."

"Oh," Bradley said. "That sounds fun." But he said it in this weird way—as if fun wasn't a great thing. Of course, then I realized that I hadn't told him that the whole point of making the film was for the cats.

"We're going to make money from the advertising," I went on, expecting to wow him with my smart thinking. "Then we'll never have to worry about running out of kibble again!"

But instead of seeming amazed by how I'd solved all our problems and come up with a new @Cat film idea in one fell swoop, Bradley just bounced his ball again. This time it got away and rolled under the flowers in someone's garden. He had to dig around to retrieve it—which seemed to take ages.

"We'll even make enough to buy supplies to build the cat shelter in my backyard," I explained, once he'd come back to the sidewalk. "Don't you think it's a great idea?"

INVENTION IDEA:

A super-bouncy ball with built-in homing device. Never lose your ball in a bush again!

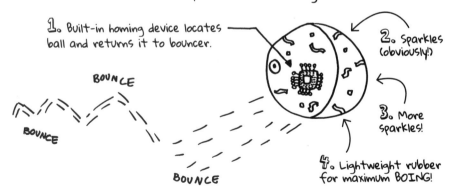

1. Built-in homing device locates ball and returns it to bouncer.

BOUNCE
BOUNCE
BOUNCE

2. Sparkles (obviously!)

3. More sparkles!

4. Lightweight rubber for maximum BOING!

Bradley fixed his gaze on a nearby bush. "Yeah. I mean, maybe. It's just, Stuart has all those videos online, and I don't think he makes any money from them."

Bradley's mom's boyfriend had made some motivational internet videos. They were called *Stuart's Six Secrets to Success*. But even though the advice in them was solid, they were pretty dull. It was just Stuart standing in front of a white background, talking in his "inspiration voice."

"This is a totally different thing," I pointed out. "Everyone knows cat videos rule the internet. And this'll be the best of the best."

"Okay," Bradley said. "I guess."

We walked on in silence for a while, except for the *boing* of Bradley half-heartedly bouncing his ball every few steps.

Finally, it was Shane who spoke up—and for once, it wasn't to complain that he was hot or tired or bored. "I was thinking," he said. "For scene six, where the super-kittens are in training, instead of filming it straight through, let's do a montage."

"A montage," I repeated, like I was thinking it over. I'd heard the word before, but I didn't know exactly what it meant. I was relieved when Bradley asked—especially because Shane gave him a look that was all like, duh!

"It's when you show short parts of different scenes," Shane explained with great authority. "And in between you have things like the sun going up and down or a clock ticking, so everyone gets that time is passing."

"Oh, right," Bradley said as we reached the churchyard fence. "I knew that."

We looked both ways and then ducked inside.

When we reached the back of the church, Shane stretched out across the dead-guy bench and started to play one of his phone games, but I got straight to work. I dropped my backpack, opened the door to the Caboodle, and peered in. Izzy-B and the kittens were piled up in a heap, fast asleep.

"Wakey-wakey," I said, lifting Peary out and setting him on the ground beside me. He blinked dozily. "We've got work to do!" I said to Pickle, putting him beside his brother. "Come on, Izzy-B," I coaxed. The mother cat hissed at me before closing her eyes again. I decided to let her sleep a little longer. We didn't need her for the next scene anyway.

"Can you pass me the kitten capes?" I asked Bradley. "They're in my backpack."

He dug out the costumes and frowned as he handed them over. "Do they like wearing those?" he asked.

It was a silly question. Seconds after I put her cape on, Twinkle Nose was rolling around in the dirt, acting like it was trying to attack her. Meanwhile, Rosie tugged at Bouncer's cape with her teeth.

"Sometimes stars need to make sacrifices," I explained calmly. I picked Twinkle Nose up and set her on her feet. Then I straightened her cape— or tried to. She bit my hand, but it didn't hurt. The kittens would be turning three weeks old the next day. They'd be growing teeth anytime now, but hers hadn't come in yet. "It's all part of showbiz."

Once everyone was in costume, we got to work on the montage. Scene six, part one involved the kittens walking across the balance beam of the Caboodle's obstacle course as they trained to become super-cats.

"I'll shoot it from underneath," Shane suggested.

"So it'll look higher." I nodded—all casual-like—but truly, I was impressed. Shane really did have a knack for this stuff. I wasn't sure I would have thought of that myself.

He lay on his back in a patch of weeds with his cell phone while I got Twinkle Nose into position at the end of the beam. It was only about two feet off the ground, but the board was long and narrow.

"Aaaaaand … action!"

I ran around to position myself at the other end. Then I took a piece of sparkly ribbon out of my pocket and started to wiggle it like an especially energetic snake. I'd been working on the kittens' training in any spare moment I could find. The sparkle snake game worked about a quarter of the time, but they were still pretty easily distracted.

Thankfully, Twinkle Nose caught sight of it. She crouched and then crept forward on her still-shaky legs. "Come on," I coaxed softly, waving the ribbon even more wildly. She scrambled for a second but made a recovery by digging her claws into the wood. She was doing great. Then a gust of wind blew a tall weed up against her tail. She startled and teetered from side to side.

"It's okay," Bradley shouted. "I've got her!" He leaped into the shot just in time to scoop up the wobbly kitten and totally ruin the scene.

Never fur! I will cat-ch you!

Totally unnecessary kitten rescue.

"Bradley! Jeez!" Shane yelled. "Get out of the way!"

"But—" Bradley held the kitten against his T-shirt. He was blinking fast behind his glasses. "She was going to fall."

"Exactly," Shane said with a sigh.

I explained it patiently. After all, not everyone's a natural when it comes to moviemaking.

"For the montage, we need to start with the kittens not being able to do the super-cat things. Then we show them learning how as it goes along. Get it?"

"Oh." Bradley bit his lip. "Sorry. I just ... forgot."

Bradley detached Twinkle Nose's claws from his

T-shirt and passed her over so I could place her back at the start of the balance beam.

"Okay, take two," Shane said, arranging himself on the ground with his phone again. "Aaaaaand … action."

"Oh!" Bradley said as Twinkle Nose started to wobble again. "Be careful!" He gasped as the kitten took another teetery-tottery step.

"Cut." Shane groaned. He hit pause on his phone. "Would you be quiet? I can't work under these conditions." He said that last part in my direction, as if he expected me to solve the problem. And, since I was the producer, it was up to me. Thankfully, I had an idea.

"Bradley," I said. "If you're not too busy, I have a really important job for you."

It was how my mom handled things when I got in her way. It used to work like a charm, but lately I'd been starting to catch on.

Thankfully, Bradley wasn't as familiar with the technique.

"Sure," he said. "How can I help?"

"It's a big responsibility."

"I can handle it," he said.

"Every movie set needs a professional Runner."

"What's that?" Bradley asked.

"It's the person who gets things to help look after the cast and crew. Or, in our case, cats and crew."

It was basically the lowest-level job on a movie set, but Bradley didn't need to know that. And anyway, it really was important in a way. "It's essential," I went on. "Without the Runner, things would fall apart."

"Oh," Bradley seemed to consider this information. "Okay."

"Izzy-B's going to be working hard and it's so hot out. She needs fresh water." I grabbed the yogurt container we used as a water dish. "Can you go fill this at the fountain in the park?"

"Sure," Bradley said.

"Cool." I saluted him. "Let's try Peary now, okay?" I said, turning my attention back to Shane. "Then we'll move on to the flaming-hoops trick."

According to my watch, it was almost six thirty. We had only half an hour left before it would be time to head home.

Bradley stopped in his tracks. "Flaming hoops?"

"Not really," I reassured him. The hoops the kittens would (hopefully) be jumping through were inflatable pool rings I'd brought from home. Shane was just going to make them look like they were on fire at the editing stage. But Bradley didn't know that, since he'd been at camp all day. And even though I wanted to explain it, I didn't really have time. "Don't worry about it, okay?" I said. "It's all under control."

Except at just that moment, I heard a rustling noise coming from my backpack, which was lying open on the ground. I caught a glimpse of whiskers poking out and ran over to find Rosie and Bouncer inside, shredding some papers with their tiny but deathly sharp claws.

"No! Not the personalized superhero crests!" I wailed. I'd drawn each one by hand the night before. It had taken forever, and @Cat was supposed to award them to the kittens in the very next scene!

I lifted the naughty kittens out and examined the crests, which were—mostly—intact, and then I turned to thank Bradley for getting the water, but his back was to us already, and he was walking away through the weeds.

Cat-astrophe Strikes

Over the next few days, I worked my buns off. Meanwhile, Shane ate snacks and played games on his phone between scenes, and Izzy-B and the kittens were less than purr-fessional about the whole acting business.

Basically, I was trying to do the job of ten people, and it was the hardest I'd ever worked in my life.

(And this is coming from a girl who once—in a single afternoon—made and hopped a hopscotch board that stretched around four city blocks.)

So it was a little frustrating that, even after dinner when he was home from JTT, Bradley didn't seem to want to pitch in. After all, it was for the good of the kittens!

On the second evening of filming, I put Bradley in charge of props. All he had to do was blow up some long balloons that I could use to make Poodle Noodle (who, in the movie, was being played by a real balloon-animal poodle tied to a string). But the kittens kept pouncing on the villain and popping him, and after inflating a third replacement, Bradley said he was too dizzy and went to sit down.

On day three, I appointed him Head of Set Design. I wanted to cover the Caboodle with black streamers and Halloween decorations so we could use it as Poodle Noodle's secret lair ... but Bradley got frustrated the second time Peary and Twinkle Nose ripped down the fake cobwebs and ran away with them. After that, he wandered into another part of the churchyard with his metal detector while Shane and I worked.

To make matters worse, the kittens kept disappearing into the tall grass right before their scenes, and Izzy-B had developed a serious grasshopper obsession. Every time she spotted one, she'd bound after it, pinning it down with her paw and then leaping up in the air to catch it when it sprang free. I tried everything—from kibble to bits of pork chop—but she refused to focus.

On day four, production got completely rained out ... and by day five, we were well behind schedule—a fact I did not need to be reminded of, but Bradley reminded me all the same.

"There are less than two bowlfuls of kibble left," he said that night, when he joined us at the churchyard after dinner. He was peering into the food container with a worried expression. "Is your movie almost finished?"

While Shane was busy playing games on his phone again, I was single-handedly wrangling six kittens and one cranky mother cat into their costumes for the big fight scene. I grabbed Bouncer and Rosie and put them into the Caboodle, where they'd be contained until I got Peary ready.

"And don't forget we're also going to need that special kitten food soon," Bradley added.

I put another caped kitten into the Caboodle and then started looking for Izzy-B, who had taken off in hot pursuit of another grasshopper. I finally spotted her near the church. By now, our star was familiar with the pre-filming routine. I hid the costume behind my back as I tiptoed toward her, but the cat had a sixth sense. As if tuning in to the antenna's presence, she put her ears back, hissed, and darted past me toward a patch of prickle weeds, where she knew I couldn't reach her. "Catch her!" I said to Bradley as she dashed past him, but he didn't even try.

And that was when I lost my patience. I was hot, I was tired, and I'd had it up to here with unhelpful kids and cats. "Thanks a lot!" I said, throwing my hands in the air.

"Sor-ry," Bradley mumbled, in a way that sounded anything but.

"What was that?" I challenged, putting my hands on my hips.

"I said sorry," he repeated, a little more sincerely this time.

"Are you going to help?" I asked. "Or are you just going to stand around twiddling your thumbs and complaining that we're not filming fast enough?"

In the past, when I'd get mad at him for something, Bradley usually reacted the same way. First, he'd get really quiet, and then before long he'd apologize, if what had happened was his fault in any way—which this time it definitely was. But yet again, I was forgetting this wasn't the old Bradley I was dealing with.

"Twiddling my thumbs?" Bradley said angrily. He banged the lid back onto the cat food box and got to his feet so that we were face to face. "For your information, I spent my whole day trying to help these kittens."

"How?" I shot back. "By searching for buried treasure?"

"Partly," he said—which didn't make any sense, but I forgot all about that as soon as he finished his sentence. "But also I've been looking for homes for them."

"You've been WHAT?!"

At the sound of our raised voices, Shane looked up from his phone and made a pained face. "Oh, man. Leave me out of this one," he said, as if we'd invited him to contribute an opinion or something!

"Looking for homes," Bradley repeated once Shane had gone back to staring at his phone. "There are two girls at camp—Joanne and Sakura. They both want a kitten. And Nelson's Persians are getting pretty old. He might be allowed to have one now. And if one of his older cats dies soon, he can probably take two. He wants Peary for sure, because he likes white cats, and maybe Pickle. So that just leaves two kittens, and Spike."

As he talked, I found myself pulling my shoulders back and puffing out my chest to look bigger and fiercer. And if I'd had fur, trust me, it would have been standing on end.

I reached down and grabbed Peary, who'd escaped from the Caboodle, and held him protectively against my chest as I hissed out the words "You are not giving my kittens away." I narrowed my eyes at Bradley. "Especially not Peary! And never to Nelson!"

"Your kittens?" Bradley said. "I thought they were *our* kittens. And in case you're forgetting,

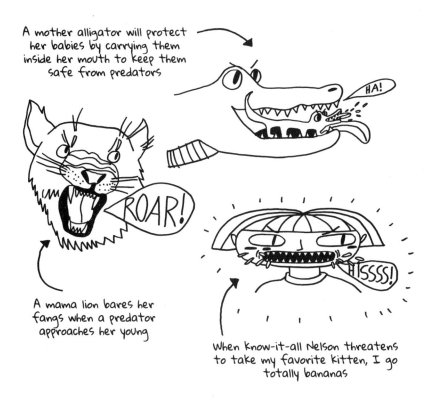

A mother alligator will protect her babies by carrying them inside her mouth to keep them safe from predators

A mama lion bares her fangs when a predator approaches her young

When know-it-all Nelson threatens to take my favorite kitten, I go totally bananas

I've paid for all their food so far. Anyway, you barely know Nelson! Why are you so against him?"

I glowered at Bradley. I didn't need to know Nelson well to be against him. The way he and JTT had slowly but surely been taking over my best friend's life was enough. But I wasn't about to let Bradley change the subject like that.

"Forget Nelson. We agreed not to tell ANYONE about the kittens," I pointed out. "And then you go and tell ALL your camp friends?"

"Yeah," Bradley answered, like it was obvious. "Because we're running out of time! Don't you think it's way better if we find them good homes ourselves? If we end up having to tell our parents about them, the kittens are going to end up at Animal Services, locked up in cages."

"No, they're not!" I yelled. "Because, like I already told you, I'm adopting them. I just need a little more time to convince my parents. You said I could have two weeks to figure it out, and it's only been one!"

Bradley sighed heavily. "Clara, be reasonable," he said in his new, irritating adult way. "Your parents are never going to say yes to that. And you know the cat family can't live in a wooden shack forever."

Pickle and Bouncer, who'd also escaped from the Caboodle, were busy swatting at some of the black streamers.

"Oh, so now you're calling the Caboodle a shack?" My voice was shaking.

Bradley sighed. "I know we did our best, but look at it!"

I did look at the Caboodle, but I didn't see what Bradley was seeing. I mean, sure, there were nails sticking out in places, and not all the boards were perfectly straight, but if I were a cat, I'd be happy to live there.

Then Bradley went and said something even more traitorous.

"And there's this whole movie thing." He wrinkled his nose, like something smelled. "It's a bad idea."

I felt like I'd just been punched in the stomach, then trampled by elephants, and then thrown off a cliff.

"Be serious. You're probably not going to make enough for cat food. At least, not in time. And I'm completely out of money now."

I glared at him, but he just kept talking—making it worse.

"I don't think your movie's going to turn out the way you're picturing it anyway. I mean, the last one didn't."

I gasped out loud. Had Bradley really just insulted @*Cat: The Movie*—a film I'd devoted a full week of my life to making?!

"I don't mean it wasn't good." He backpedaled. "But it was barely thirty seconds long. It wasn't exactly a real movie."

It was twenty-three seconds, but in stop-motion animation, that was about nine thousand frames. He didn't know the first thing about what it took to make a feature film!

Bradley looked down at his feet. "I'm just saying, there are probably easier ways to raise money for cat food."

"Oh yeah? Like what?" I yelled.

By then, Shane had given up on his game and was ping-ponging his head back and forth, watching our argument.

"You think you're soooo mature, don't you? You think you know everything." I glared at Bradley. "Ever since you turned ten, you barely want to do anything fun anymore. Well, if you don't believe in our movie, just go home!" I said. "It's not like you're helping anyway. Just go hang out with your precious camp friends instead."

At first, Bradley blinked fast behind his glasses, like he was trying not to cry, but then he got a cold, hard look in his eye. "Fine," he said. "I will. At least they appreciate me!" He picked up his metal detector.

"And stay away!" I went on. "Shane and I don't need you. And neither do the cats. I'll take care of them myself."

He glared at me angrily, but I wasn't finished. "And don't think you're getting your name in the movie credits," I added. "Because you're not."

But if Bradley cared, he didn't let it show. Instead, he switched on his metal detector and swept it angrily through the weeds on his way out.

Cat Fight

Bradley and I had been backyard neighbors and best friends our whole lives, so obviously, in all that time, we'd had our share of troubles. For example, there was the mess we got ourselves into when I thought I had (incredibly minor) super powers, and the time we got caught up in a boys-versus-girls battle and I did one or two things that were less than noble. But when you got right down to it, those were misunderstandings. This was our first time not even being friends anymore. And as far as I was concerned, it was permanent.

The things Bradley had said and done were just plain unforgivable. Trying to give away the kittens was bad enough, but then insulting the Caboodle and my film on top of that? I'd put my heart and soul into both of those things ... and if they weren't good enough for Bradley, then neither was I.

In fact, every time I thought about what he'd said

and done, my teeth got all clenchy, tears sprang to my eyes, and my heart raced. I was so upset that it took me ages to get to sleep that night, and I woke up Saturday morning squeezing handfuls of bedsheet in my fists. My parents asked what was wrong when I slammed a box of Cheerios down on the counter and sloshed the milk all over the place, but I just mumbled "Nothing."

Obviously, I couldn't tell them. And anyway, I needed to focus my energy where it was needed most: on finishing the best internet cat film ever made, saving the cat family, and proving Bradley wrong, all at the same time.

As soon as I was done breakfast, I asked if I could go to Shane's. That morning, we started by reviewing what he'd put together so far. Besides the insanely awesome opening credits, the first few scenes were also complete. It was looking good. So good, in fact, that even though I knew it was coming, I found myself wiping a tear from my eye when, in scene five, @Cat came across the poor abandoned kittens and, one by one, tenderly licked them clean with her super-spit.

Fueled by a loaf of Janet's extremely excellent

banana bread, we got busy editing and made it all the way to the climax that day. (That's film-industry speak for "the part of the movie that makes you nearly pee your pants in excitement.") Would Poodle Noodle succeed in his plan to hypnotize @Cat and turn her into his Agent of Evil?

@CAT and the UNSTOPPABLE 6

Will the super-kittens, still so young and inexperienced, find a way to rise to the challenge and save the day?

I won't ruin it by telling you what happens—but I will say this: Never underestimate how cunning cuddly kittens can be.

On Sunday, we added some professional touches, like cool special effects and suspense-building music, but even though we were close, we weren't quite done. We had to head back to the churchyard on Monday morning to film one last scene: The one where the kittens fly off into the sunset toward their next great adventure. We did it by having them leap, one by one, off the seat of the dead-guy bench while I held a blue bedsheet in the background to represent the sky. The kittens did great (most of them even landed on their feet), and when Shane added the sunset in with special effects, it would look fantastic.

All the same, there was a big problem: When I'd checked the food container before we left for home, there'd only been crumbs of kibble left for Izzy-B. She was still nursing the kittens, and if she didn't eat, it was only a matter of time before she wouldn't have enough milk for them.

Bradley had been dead wrong. The movie had turned out better than even I could have imagined. And I knew that the second Shane uploaded it to the internet that night, it was going to make a ton of money I could use to help animals in need ... but it wasn't going to happen soon enough. It was time to admit it: I needed to think of another way to get cat food. And fast.

Thankfully, a pound of melted butter saved the day.

"Andrew!" my mom complained. She'd just picked up the butter dish from the picnic table. A thin, oily stream dripped down the side. "You left the butter sitting out in the sun again."

"Oh. Sorry," Dad said absently. He set a bowl of salad on the patio table ... but even I could tell he was busy eyeing the deck, making a to-do list in his mind.

"You forgot to do the laundry too," Mom went on. "And you know Clara's almost out of clean shirts."

"Oh, that's right," Dad said, still distracted. "I'll put in a load after dinner."

"What you need to do is get this deck done," Mom went on, following his gaze. "It has you completely distracted. Not to mention that it's costing a fortune."

I hated when they argued. And I especially hated when they argued about the deck, since the missing supplies were my fault. "I'll go with Bradley and get more butter from Andy's store after dinner," I offered, to soothe my mom. She still didn't know about our big fight, which worked to my advantage, since she probably wouldn't let me go if she knew I'd be going alone.

"Sure. Thanks, Clara," she said, but then she
went right back to worrying aloud about the price
of lumber—so I was relieved when, after clearing
the plates, I had a reason to excuse myself from the
table, especially because I'd just come up with a
way to solve my cat food problem.

The shop bells jangled softly when I pushed
open the door of the Milk 'n' Variety. And—like
always—Andy grinned when he saw it was me.

"Clara!" He reached over and lowered the volume
on the little TV he kept behind the counter. "What
can I getcha?"

"Butter," I answered, leaning against the counter.
"A pound of your finest."

"Coming right up," Andy said. "But first ..." he
squinted mischievously, so I knew it was going to
be another good one, "riddle me this: What goes
up but never comes down?"

I stroked my chin thoughtfully, like a Puzzle
Scientist or a Professor of Riddles might do if

those were real jobs, which they totally should be. (Solving riddles takes skills and smarts—especially when they're Andy's riddles.)

Hot-air balloons, birds, and the price of gas: Those things went up ... but even that last one sometimes came down. (My dad always rushed to fill up the car and the lawn mower when it did.)

Helicopters ... the hair on the back of your neck when you sense trouble brewing ... your hand when you totally know the answer ... None of those was right either, though.

"Give up?" Andy said.

"Never!" I announced. "But let me get back to you."

Riddles could wait. It was time to put my "get cat food pronto" plan into action. I reached into my pocket, took out a piece of paper, unfolded it, and slid it across the counter to Andy.

That afternoon, while Shane had been working on the last of the video edits, I'd had a brain wave. Now that @Cat had a litter of super-kittens at her disposal, and they'd successfully captured Poodle Noodle in a cinematic tour-de-force that was going to be uploaded to the internet that very night, there was no reason to stop!

"What's this?" Andy said, putting on his reading glasses. "Your new film idea?"

"Yup," I said proudly. "It's going to be a brand-new @Cat movie. Not Claymation though. I'm going to film it using real cats."

He raised his eyebrows a little, so I quickly added, "Momo's cats. Next time I visit her."

Obviously, he knew Momo and her cats from when she'd lived on our street.

"In this one," I explained, "@Cat harnesses the power of stray kittens all around the world. See," I said, really getting into my pitch now, "she discovers that by feeding kittens a special kind of food, she can give them super powers. Then she realizes that if she can make every stray kitten in the world into a super-cat, there'll be no stopping her power to do good."

"Well, now." Andy leaned forward to study the storyboard more closely. "Sounds like an uplifting story."

"Oh, it is," I promised. "Only ..." I made sad eyes. "I might not be able to make it. I don't have a budget for props. You know, like the cat food. I'm going to need a big bag of cat food for filming. So I can pretend it's super-cat food."

I waited ... hoping ... but Andy didn't go for it right away.

"Why let that stop you?" he said. "You just get yourself a bag of something—potatoes from your mom and dad's kitchen, say—and then write 'super-cat food' on it."

I grimaced and tried another tactic.

"That's a good idea, but I don't know." I sighed. "This is going to be a high-quality movie. I want it to look just right. Remember that bag of cat food you sold us before? For

Stuart's cat? That one was perfect ... except the cat already ate it and Bradley's mom threw out the packaging," I added quickly.

Finally, Andy took the bait. "Oh. Well," he said, "if that's the one you want, you go ahead and borrow a bag. As long as you don't open it. Just bring it back when you're done."

"Really?!" I said with a look of perfect surprise. "That would be amazing. Only ..." I trailed off, looking a little hopeless again. I slid the storyboard back toward myself and folded it up. "I also need some kitten food. Just for one of the scenes. You don't have any of that, do you?"

"Why don't we take a look?" Andy said.

So even though I didn't manage to solve the riddle about what goes up but never comes down, I still walked out of Andy's store victorious that day, with a bag of kitty kibble in my arms, as well as three cans of kitten food and a pound of butter dangling from my wrist in a plastic bag. And all for free (except for the butter). Or on loan, anyway. I was obviously going to pay Andy back as soon as the first live-action @Cat film went viral.

Andy had even thrown in a licorice whip, which I was holding in my mouth. It flopped around as I skipped the whole way to the churchyard, despite the heavy stuff I was holding. But when I reached the gate, I stopped cold. Because there, towering above the "Private Property," "Danger!" and "Trespassers Will Be Prosecuted" warnings, was a brand-new sign—and it was more terrifying than all the old ones combined.

"Oh no!" someone said. I jumped and turned to see Bradley standing behind me.

"What are you doing here?" I snapped.

But he didn't answer. He was too busy reading the sign. Also, he was probably still too mad to talk to me. Which was fine. I was way too mad at him too.

In fact, I was about to tell him that if he was there to get the kittens he'd promised his camp friends, he was going to have to get through me first … but then I noticed that he was looking past me and that he'd gone pale. I followed his gaze. The metal gate (which had always been locked before) was partway open.

That was when I heard the murmuring of voices.

"Six stories … mm-hmm … parking …" I only managed to catch a few snippets, spoken in a deep tone. I walked closer to the fence and peered in. Some of the weeds near the center of the churchyard were swaying. Two yellow hard hats appeared. They bobbed around like beach balls on top of waves as the people wearing them talked. "No reason we can't apply for a permit for that," one of the men said.

Then the bobbing hats started moving again,

toward the far side of the lot—right in the direction of the Caboodle!

"Oh no!" I whispered.

But whether it was because he didn't care about the kittens, because he didn't care about me, or both, Bradley stood frozen to the spot. If anyone was going to save the day, it was going to have to be me.

Luckily, creating a distraction in a tricky situation is Superhero 101 kind of stuff. There was the well-timed stink-bomb explosion and, of course, the double-hero tag-team approach.

Unfortunately, I didn't have any stink bombs, and sadder still, I'd lost my sidekick. I was going to have to employ a third—but no less powerful—technique.

The time @Cat and her friend Sly Fox used the "Foxy Lady" distraction technique to outwit Poodle Noodle.

I sat down on the sidewalk.

"Heeeeeelp!" I started shouting. "Help meeeeee!"

Bradley stared at me like I'd lost my mind.

"I need a grown-up!" I made my voice sound especially pitiful. "Heeeeeelp!"

"Clara," Bradley whispered. "What are you doing?"

"The damsel in distress," I whispered back. "Look, you don't have to help, but at least don't wreck it."

Bradley crouched on the sidewalk beside me, looking fake-concerned—which was better than nothing, but not by a lot. Just then, a door across the street opened, and a lady with gray hair walked out onto her porch.

"Great," I said under my breath. My cries had attracted the wrong person, and for a second, all hope seemed lost, but then I heard the swishing sounds of weeds parting behind us. The men in the churchyard were approaching as well.

"Everything okay, kids?" the lady called out as she looked both ways to cross the street.

"Um, yeah. We're fine," Bradley said, but I wasn't about to give up until the kittens were safe. I kept right on crying. The gate creaked open and a tall man wearing one of the yellow hats poked his head out.

"I think she's hurt herself," the lady explained to him as they both reached us. She bent down beside me, wincing a little like Momo did when her knees felt stiff from too much gardening. "You all right, sweetie?" she asked gently.

"No," I said, sniffing. "I fell." Then I pointed to my leg. While I'd been wailing and waiting for an adult to come to my rescue, I'd ripped off the dirty Band-Aids that had been covering my road-rashed and cat-scratched shin. Then, quick as a flash, I'd picked at the new scab that was just starting to heal until it came loose. The injury looked almost as fresh as the day I'd first fallen off my bike, and there was an impressive amount of blood.

"Would you like me to get you a bandage for that?" the lady asked.

Instead of answering, I started crying all over again. Even louder. Like I couldn't even bear the thought.

"It's okay, kid. Don't cry. I've got a first-aid kit in my truck," the hard-hat man offered. "It won't hurt a bit." And then I actually did stop crying, because I caught sight of his friend stepping out from inside the gates to see what was happening. My plan had worked! They were both safely away from the kittens.

"Okay," I said with a small sniff. The first man went to his truck for the first-aid kit while his co-worker stayed with me and Bradley, and the old lady went home to get me a glass of water. Then, when I was all patched up and had gulped down the water, one of the men helped me to my feet. I heard him say something to his friend about quitting time. They both got in the truck and drove away.

"Where do you two live?" the old woman asked. When I told her it was just around the corner and up two blocks, she insisted on walking me and Bradley home.

It turned out that her name was Nancy, and as we walked, she chatted about how the plants could use some more rain; and how many trees had come down in the big ice storm the winter before; how lovely that little house on the corner was with its robin's-egg-blue front door; and look at that squirrel's big, bushy tail—and aren't squirrels funny, the way they chase each other?

In fact, Nancy talked so much that neither Bradley nor I could get a word in—which was fine, since I didn't want to talk to him anyway. Also, it gave me time to think. We were only a block from my house and I had a big (cat-food-bag-shaped) problem on my hands. If I showed up at my front door with kibble and cans of kitten food, my parents were sure to have questions.

I ... um ... love the meaty crunch of tuna and beef ...

Aren't you a vegetarian now?

KITTY KIBBLE

Oh yeah ...

"Stash it there," Bradley whispered— almost as if he were reading my mind. He motioned with his head to a mailbox we were approaching.

I eyed him suspiciously. If we weren't friends anymore (and we sure didn't seem to be) and he didn't believe in me and my movie (he'd made that much clear), why was he trying to help? Obviously, I figured it out a second later. He wanted to keep the kittens healthy. How else was he going to give them away to his precious camp friends?

All the same, he was right. There weren't going to be any other good hiding places between there and my house. It was behind the mailbox or nothing.

While Nancy was busy showing Bradley how to open and close the mouth of a flower called a snapdragon to make it look like it was talking, I quietly dropped the supplies.

A minute later, we were standing on my porch. Nancy rang the doorbell.

"Oh, hello." Mom sounded surprised and a bit worried.

Nancy explained how I'd fallen and she'd wanted to see me and Bradley home. Then the adults did thank-you's and nice-to-meet-you's, but I barely listened. My mind was racing with all that had just happened and all that might happen next … because, sure, my fake-hurt leg had kept the builders from discovering the Caboodle for the moment, but they'd be back, and there was no telling what they might do with the kittens.

"Clara!" my mom scolded. "What do you say?"

"About what?" I asked.

"To Nancy? For bringing you home?"

"Oh, thanks," I muttered.

"You're quite welcome, dear," Nancy said. Then she frowned. "Oh! Your parcel. What's happened to it? You had a parcel with you when you fell." I just stood there blinking. "You must have left it on the sidewalk."

"That would be the butter she picked up for me at Andy's store," my mom said. "Not a problem. We'll go get more later."

"But there was something else." Nancy seemed to be searching her memory.

I held my breath, certain I was about to get busted, but at that exact moment, Mr. Johansson across the street fired up his noisy lawn mower. "It was cat food," Nancy said, but her words were mostly drowned out.

"What's that?" Mom asked.

"Cat food," Nancy repeated.

My mother looked puzzled, but she must have assumed she'd misheard. "Oh, okay then," she yelled. "Well, thanks again for bringing the kids home."

And with that, Nancy smiled, waved, and turned for home.

The Three Disasters

I had another restless night's sleep—this time worrying about the cats and the condo builders. First thing in the morning (under the guise of walking to the mailbox to send Momo a postcard with otters on the front), I dashed out to retrieve the kibble.

But before I could even drop the postcard into the mailbox, I yelped. Disaster had struck (and it wouldn't be the only—or even the worst—disaster that day). I felt like kicking myself for not having foreseen it.

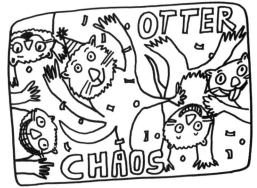

It's been a crazy summer! I'll tell you all about it when you visit for Halloween.

Miss you!!!!!

♡ CLARA xoxo

TO: MOMO

1445 FOREST WAY

BOWMANVILLE 34487

P.S. Bring cat treats. (I'll explain later.)

The plastic bag from Andy's store had been ripped to shreds. The butter was completely gone (except for a few scraps of the foil packaging), and the kibble bag had been torn wide open, its contents devoured by raccoons … exactly the same thing that had happened to our first bag! All that remained were the tins of kitten food. I scooped them up and ran home.

My next thought was to find meat for Izzy-B. Any kind. I searched our fridge, but since I was vegetarian, we didn't have any of the salami I used to like … and all the chicken and steak was frozen solid. I knew Bradley's mom always had this mushy pâté that she smeared on crackers. It would make perfect cat food, but going there for help wasn't an option.

There was one last hope. I ran over to knock on Shane's door. It was nine thirty. Janet was still in her pajamas, and Shane was in bed.

"Wake up, wake up, wake up!" I said, pounding on his bedroom door—which Janet let me do because she didn't want him sleeping all day.

"What're you doing here?" Shane asked blearily.

He was wearing jammies with skateboarding dinosaurs on them.

"We have to check on our film." I pushed past him and sat down in front of his computer. "You uploaded it, right?"

He nodded and rubbed at his eyes.

"Show me the link."

Shane barely grumbled, and he leaned over the keyboard and started typing right away—so I could tell even he was excited.

We waited a hundred years while the page loaded, and then sat through an ad for floor cleaner. (But I didn't mind. It was making us money!) Finally, there was our film: live on the internet in all its glory! The intro music began with its heavy bass line and a picture of Izzy-B as @Cat flashed onto the screen.

Even though I'd seen it all before, I was instantly captivated. We laughed. We cringed. I even caught Shane getting misty-eyed during the part where Twinkle Nose paws lovingly at @Cat's face. We watched the whole two and a half minutes, right through to the triumphant final scene and end credits, barely taking a breath. Then I scrolled down to the bottom of the page to check our views and revenue. That was the second disaster.

Page views: 4
Earnings: 0.004 cents
VIDEOS UP NEXT:
Fierce & Fluffy: Big tails, bigger cattitudes.
Puss 'N' Toots: The amazing adventures of a flatulent feline.

So far, we had four video views—and one of those had been us.

"What?! How can we have made only four cents?" I cried.

"Umm," Shane said. "That's actually four-tenths of a cent. See the decimal point?"

I groaned. Then I glanced nervously at Shane.

The only thing that had been keeping him quiet about the cat family had been the promise of money—lots of it. But he wasn't making any move to run to his mom and tell on me. At least, not yet.

"It's probably because there are so many videos

like ours." Shane pointed out the links at the bottom of the screen.

Obviously, I'd known there were plenty of cat videos on the internet ... but I'd figured we'd at least be in the top ten for live-action super-cat videos. Wrong! Toast Cat (a cat who wore a piece of toast on his head while fighting crime) had about twenty episodes all on its own—all with thousands of views. I clicked on a few of them, and each one was more action-packed and hilarious than the last! How were we supposed to compete with that?!

"Don't sweat it," Shane said kindly, which took me completely by surprise. "Quality has a way of rising to the top. It just might take a while. We'll check back later."

Toast Cat, our (adorable) internet nemesis.

But when I told him about the condo-development sign and the men who'd been tromping around the churchyard, even he looked concerned. Then, when I mentioned how the cat food I'd borrowed from Andy's store had been gobbled up by raccoons, Shane Biggs did something that outright shocked me.

"Mooooom!" he called.

"Yes," Janet yelled back from her office.

"Can you make me something with meat?"

"Something with meat?" she yelled back.

"Yeah. Like bacon and sausages or something."

And because Janet is the kindest sort of mother, within half an hour, Shane's house was filled with the heavenly smell of bacon frying. I'm ashamed to admit that I was hoping Janet would forget I was vegetarian—just so I could have a small taste—but when we walked into the kitchen, she already had a place set for me with cereal and juice.

"Actually, I'll take it to go." Shane was already wrapping the bacon up in a paper towel. "We'll be at the park, okay?"

Janet said that was fine, and so, with a doggie

bag (or should I say kitty bag?) in hand, we were soon on our way to feed Izzy-B.

And that was when the third (and most upsetting) disaster struck.

We were a block from the churchyard when Shane tugged on my sleeve. "Look," he said.

On the other side of the road and halfway down the block stood Bradley. He was easy to spot because of his bright-orange JTT hat.

I shielded my eyes with one hand and squinted into the sun.

"What's he doing?"

He was stopped near a telephone pole and he appeared to be taping some kind of blue poster to it. He had an old red wagon that had seen better days. I recognized it—even from a distance—as mine. Inside it was a large cardboard box. But the fact that my former best friend was a wagon thief wasn't even close to being the worst part!

Shane tapped me on the shoulder. He pointed to the lamppost nearest to us. There, freshly attached with clear tape, was a poster the exact same shade of blue as the ones Bradley was putting up.

The Poster of Absolute Betrayal.

My heart started pounding double time. "Oh no," I said. "He's not getting away with this."

I grabbed the poster and ripped it down, and then marched to the next lamppost and did the same.

"Bradley!" I called, but he seemed to be in his own little world. I watched as he finished taping up one more poster and then pulled the wagon around the corner—no doubt headed for the churchyard to collect the kittens so he could give some of them to his camp friends and the rest to complete strangers!

"Bradley!" I yelled again. I broke into a run. A second later, I heard Shane's sandals pounding the pavement behind me, but by the time we rounded the corner, Bradley had already abandoned the red wagon by the fence and disappeared through the hole.

I was about to lift the broken fencing to slip through behind him when I felt a hand on my shoulder. "Clara. Wait." Shane was looking down the block. There, at the stop sign near the corner, was a large yellow bulldozer. It turned and headed toward us, stopping in front of the locked gate.

"They're going in," Shane whispered.

Sure enough, a man in a construction vest hopped out. He undid the padlock, swung the big gate open, and directed as a second worker drove the huge machine right into the churchyard. It crunched over the gravel pathway and flattened the tall weeds in its path.

"The kittens are trapped," Shane said breathlessly.

"And so is Bradley," I added in a shaky voice.

The Unstoppable 3

Shane and I stood outside the churchyard fence. The sun beat down on us and the seconds ticked by with agonizing slowness. We needed to do something—but what could we possibly do? If we went in after Bradley, we were sure to get caught trespassing. But as angry as I was, I couldn't just abandon Bradley ... or the cat family.

"Wait here and be the lookout," I whispered to Shane. I ducked into the churchyard through the gap in the fence.

Keeping low, I inched through the weeds, glancing over at the bulldozer. It was stopped a few feet from the fence, and the construction workers were talking, pausing every so often to take sips from takeout coffee cups. Thankfully, I knew a thing or two about adults and their morning coffee. This was going to buy me some time.

I crawled on my hands and knees toward the

Caboodle, where I knew Bradley would be.

"Aha!" I proclaimed in a whisper. I'd caught him red-handed—which, in this case, meant with a kitten in each hand, loading them into the cardboard box he'd had in the back of my wagon. "I knew you were up to no good!"

Bradley jumped, but when he saw it was just me, he went straight back to kitten-napping.

Bradley caught kitten-handed.

"Help me out, wouldja? It's only a matter of time before they drive that bulldozer behind the building—or worse, through it. We need to get them out of here."

He had a point. If we started arguing about who got to keep the kittens, soon there might not be any kittens left to keep. I grabbed Peary and placed him gently in the box.

"Fine," I whispered to Bradley. I couldn't help adding, "But don't think I don't know your plans.

I saw your little posters." In fact, I still had a bunch of them crumpled tightly in one fist. I tossed them into the box to free up my hands and then closed the flaps to contain the kittens that were already inside.

There were four: Peary, Rosie, Twinkle Nose, and Pickle—which meant we were still missing Prickle, Bouncer, and, of course, Izzy-B. I got up to search inside the Caboodle and almost tripped over some stuff Bradley had left lying in the weeds: a big bag of cat food, a tin of kitten food, and a can opener. Under normal circumstances, I might have paused to wonder where he'd gotten it all—or why—but these definitely weren't normal circumstances.

"Let's start with the rubble over there," one of the construction workers called out loudly to the other. By the sound of her voice, I could tell she was to the left of us on the other side of the building—a little too close for comfort. "Tomorrow Tom's bringing in the big equipment to start taking down the church."

As the worker was talking, I noticed a rustling in the grass behind Bradley. A little nose poked out. "Grab him!" I whispered. Bradley managed to scoop up Bouncer. Then Prickle emerged from the bushes behind her brother. I opened the flaps of the box and Bradley put them both in. Now we had all six kittens. But where on earth was their mother?

"Clara." Bradley nudged me. There she was! Izzy-B was balancing along the top of the dead-guy bench with expert grace ... exactly as she'd refused to in scene twelve of @*Cat and the Unstoppable 6*.

Tut-tut-tut. I made a soft clicking sound with my tongue, hoping to get her attention. Not surprisingly, it didn't work. "Izzy," I whispered. She didn't so much as glance my way. A grasshopper near the fence had her full focus. She was hunching up her shoulders and wiggling her bum, preparing to pounce.

I considered running over to grab her, but then I came to my senses. Izzy-B had never—not once— let me pick her up. If I tried, she'd make a dash for the prickle bushes like she did whenever I needed to put on her antenna.

Suddenly, I had an idea.

"Bradley!" I whispered. "Do you have your ball with you? The rainbow one? From JTT?"

He reached into his pocket and pulled it out. "Why?" he asked. But I didn't have time to explain.

"When I say 'now,' open the box and catch the cat," I instructed. I grabbed the ball out of his hand and crawled through the weeds as fast as I could.

"We'll need a Dumpster for that," one of the workers said to the other. "But we can pile it up for now." I could hear their footsteps retreating. There was a rumbling sound as the bulldozer started up.

I was only going to have one chance.

I stood up, took aim, and made my throw.

"Aaaaand jump, Izzy," I said softly as the bouncy ball rebounded off the seat of the bench—coming just inches from the cat's nose. Almost instantly, Izzy snapped her attention away from the grasshopper. As far as she was concerned, there was an even bigger, bouncier, brighter bug on the loose.

The cat jumped down to the seat of the bench. She pounced but missed the ball. It bounced up again—not as high as before. She came close on her next leap, but instead of trapping it between her paws like a mouse, she accidentally pushed it forward. Luckily, it went in the right direction.

"Aaaaand ... now!" I said to Bradley, who pushed the box over and opened the flaps just in time to capture the rolling ball and—seconds later—the mother cat, who followed it straight in.

"Whoa," Bradley said under his breath as he slapped the lid closed. "You actually trained her?" Then he seemed to remember what was most important. "Run," he whispered. "Take the box and run for it."

I wrapped my arms tightly around the big cardboard box, and then shifted my weight so I'd be ready to go, but when I glanced back at Bradley, he was moving in the opposite direction.

"Bradley! Aren't you coming?" I whispered furiously, but he shook his head and kept going. He was heading around to the opposite side of the church. What the heck was he thinking? I didn't have time to wait and see. I needed to move those kittens. First, I tried to lift the box, but it was too heavy—not to mention shifty, with so many cats moving around inside. Instead, I started dragging it.

When I reached the front corner of the church, I paused to catch my breath. I peered out to make sure the coast was clear of workers, and that was when I saw the whole scene.

"Ahem!"

Bradley was standing at the top of the church steps, his bright-orange JTT camp hat standing out like a beacon. Both of the workers had turned at the sound of him loudly clearing his throat.

"Hey, kid! What're you doing in here? This is private property," one of them called out. And as they started toward him, he began to talk. Still, it took me a second to realize why.

"What is private property, though?" Bradley asked. His voice was shaking, but only a little. "Doesn't this earth belong to us all?"

He was creating a distraction!

"And doesn't that include this churchyard?" Bradley went on, gaining momentum.

And even though lately I'd been less and less impressed by the many ways my best friend had been changing, in that moment, I couldn't help feeling a little proud. This wasn't just any old distraction. Bradley—the same guy who used to be too shy to raise his hand in class, even when he knew the answers—was monologuing!

One of the many times @Cat used monologuing as a defensive tactic against Poodle Noodle ...

"Look, kid. It's not safe to play in here," the worker interrupted. "That's why there are signs posted saying to keep out."

"Signs?!" Bradley faked outrage. "Signs?! And what are signs but words, arranged in a certain order?"

He was really on a roll, and part of me wanted to stay and watch, but I knew I couldn't. The workers were focused on Bradley now. If I darted left and then headed straight, I might just be able to make it out of the open gate undetected. But that would mean leaving Bradley behind ...

I glanced up at him from the spot where I was crouched in the weeds, and he met my gaze. Go! his eyes urged. Now! So I dragged the heavy, mewling box backward through the weeds, moving as fast as I could. I cut straight through a patch of prickle bushes that tore at my legs and made them sting. I skirted a pile of rubble, and then I hauled those cats right past the digger and toward the open gate.

I was nearly at the sidewalk too when: "Hey! Little girl! What're you doing in there?"

I glanced over my shoulder. Standing by the gate were two more workers who must have just arrived. One had a large droopy mustache, and the other had two pigtails sticking out from under her hard hat. They were sipping takeout coffee and blocking my path. Where had they come from? And more importantly, how was I supposed to evade them with a giant box of cats?

"You'd better not be stealing things from the

church," Pigtails said.

I wrapped my arms even more tightly around the box. I didn't know what I was going to do ... but one thing was certain: I wasn't about to just hand the kittens over.

There was a rustling in the weeds to my right. Were more workers starting to surround me? I looked over but couldn't see anyone.

"This is private property, you know," Pigtails continued. "We're going to need to see what's inside that box before we can let you leave."

By now, both the workers were approaching me, their boots making an ominous crunching noise against the gravel pathway. I hated to admit it, but I was all out of ideas.

"Here, kid ... lemme see that," Mustache said. He bent over and reached down to open up the box flaps. In a last, desperate attempt, I covered the top with my hands—not that it would do much good.

"Aaaaaahhhhhh!"

I jumped—and so did the workers—as a primitive yell pierced the air.

Someone—or something—was running toward us. It took me a few seconds to realize it was Shane

Biggs, probably
because his face
was smeared in
mud, and he was
covered from
head to toe in
weeds.

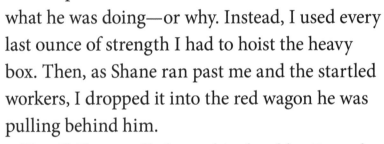

Shane-the-Bush Biggs.

"Quick, Clara.
Pick it up," he yelled.
I didn't pause to wonder
what he was doing—or why. Instead, I used every
last ounce of strength I had to hoist the heavy
box. Then, as Shane ran past me and the startled
workers, I dropped it into the red wagon he was
pulling behind him.

"Run!" Shane yelled over his shoulder. I caught a
glimpse of something clear and shiny against his
weed-covered T-shirt, and that was when I realized
what he'd done and how he'd done it. Shane must
have snuck into the churchyard after me, along
with the wagon. Not only had he been lying in wait
in case I needed his help ... he'd also used the only
materials at his disposal (Bradley's roll of packing
tape, mud, and some of the many weeds in the

churchyard) to camouflage himself. Despite the long, green stems that were dangling off his legs and arms, he had impressive speed.

"Coming!" I dashed after him, moving past Pigtails in such a flash that she spilled her coffee.

"I know a shortcut," Shane called out as he ran across the street, pulling the rickety wagonload of cats behind him.

Then my new neighbor—the least adventurous person I thought I'd ever met—led us down a shaded alleyway I'd never really noticed before, through the backyard of a startled-looking old man who was out weeding his flower box, across the parking lot, and past the dumpster behind Andy's Milk 'n' Variety, and all the way home.

Lost Cat

Me and Shane were like fugitives: on the run, with nowhere to go. Obviously, we couldn't show up at my house with a box of cats (at least, not without some serious explaining to do). And we couldn't go to Shane's either—because even though Janet would definitely let us in with the cat family, she'd also definitely tell my parents, and then I'd be right back to the serious explaining part.

In the end, the only safe place we could think of was Shane's garage, and it wouldn't be safe for long. His mom kept a freezer out there, and Shane said she went in almost every night to get stuff for dinner.

Still, it was better than nothing, and it gave us a chance to catch our breath.

I let the kittens out of the box to explore the garage. Shane fed Izzy-B bits of the bacon he still had wrapped up in a paper towel in his pocket.

Then he went inside to wash the mud off his face, tell his mom we were back, and get the cat family some fresh water.

While he was gone, I sat with the kittens and fretted. Best-case scenario: The construction workers had dragged Bradley home to Svetlana, where he'd been sent straight to his room to begin the longest grounding of his life. Worst-case: They'd called the police and had him carted off to jail, or maybe they'd even prosecuted him, like the sign on the fence promised.

I was just about to go knock on his door to check if he was home and okay when Peary batted a balled-up piece of paper against my leg, wanting to play.

"Not now, Peary," I said, but kittens aren't famous for their patience. He batted it at me again, and again. The fourth time, I picked it up.

It was one of Bradley's horrible "Free Kittens" posters. I'd nearly forgotten that I'd tossed some of them into the box. I uncrumpled it and noticed that there were actually three sheets of paper in my hand—and only the top one was Bradley's poster. I must have pulled them all off the lamppost together. I glared at Bradley's poster angrily, balled it up, and threw it hard against the garage wall.

Peary dashed after it. That got Bouncer's attention, so I balled up the second paper. It was an ad for a hot-stone massage at a local spa. Only ninety-nine dollars! Hot stones? Really? I could make those for free in the microwave. I tossed it.

But now Pickle wanted to play too, so I was about to crumple the third sheet of paper—but first, I glanced down to see what it was. And when I did, my heart nearly stopped.

LOST!

SEVEN-MONTH-OLD CAT
IF FOUND PLEASE CALL: 555-778-0808.
I MISS HER TERRIBLY!

ANSWERS TO MUFFY

Even though one corner of the poster was ripped away, the picture on it was intact. Staring up at me was a mostly white cat with gray and brown splotches, and a patch over one eye that was shaped almost exactly like a heart.

I glanced over at Izzy-B, who was napping in a corner while Rosie and Twinkle Nose nursed, and then back at the torn, faded poster ... and then back at Izzy-B. I mean, obviously there was a strong resemblance, but there were plenty of mostly white cats in the world. I couldn't really be 100 percent sure. "Isadorabella," I called, to get her attention. She kept right on sleeping. "Izzy-B," I tried. Then, just in case, "Spike."

I took a deep breath and looked down at the poster again. "Muffy," I said in barely a whisper.

The mother cat blinked her eyes open, looked straight at me, and meowed.

"Do cats like ice in their water?" Shane asked, coming back into the garage with two glasses filled to the brim. "I wasn't sure, so I put some in just in case."

"No, no, no," I said under my breath. And quickly, before he could see, I crumpled up the lost-cat poster and shoved it into my pocket.

"Jeez. All right, I'll take it out then," Shane said, popping a cube into his mouth.

We spent the rest of the afternoon in his garage. Shane got busy making up a game for Twinkle Nose that involved traffic cones and a piece of bacon tied to a string. Meanwhile, I worried about Bradley.

"I'm just going to go over for a sec," I said. "Just to make sure he got home safely."

"Uh-uh. Bad call," Shane said. "If you go, your parents might find out you were sneaking into the churchyard too. And you think they'll let you keep the kittens then?"

He had a point.

"What if I just peek in through the window?" I tried a few minutes later.

But Shane shook his head. "You'll get caught," he said, "and if you get caught, I get caught. If my mom finds out I was there, I'll lose video games for a month. Not happening."

So we sat tight, but I couldn't get Bradley out of my head. Also, I worried about the poster. If I'd lost a cat as great as Izzy-B, I knew I'd want her back—badly. But then again, I thought as I scratched Bouncer under the chin and let Peary settle in for a nap across my shoulders, judging by how faded it was, the paper had been hanging on the lamppost at least two or three months. Maybe even longer. It was possible the owner had given up on finding their cat. And did a person like that even deserve Izzy-B?

If I'd lost my chinchilla, forget putting up some measly posters! I would have sent out a search party, looked behind every bush, hired a pet detective even (if that's a thing). I wouldn't have stopped until I found her.

And when you thought about it like that, weren't Izzy-B and her kittens better off with me?

Luckily, Shane promised he'd do his best to convince his mom to order pizza that night so she wouldn't go into the garage. That bought me twenty-four hours (at most) to figure out my next move.

That night at dinner, I barely touched the mushy green-bean casserole my dad had made me (and not just because it looked like something you might find at the bottom of

a fish tank). Afterward I went upstairs to my
room without any dessert and sat miserably
by the window, staring at the back of Bradley's
house—wondering what was going on inside—
and then at Shane's garage, where the kittens
were hopefully fast asleep, chasing dandelion
fluffs in their dreams.

In fact, I sat there so miserably, and for such a
long time, that I may well have slipped into some
sort of meditative trance when, out of nowhere,
a smattering of tiny rocks hit the window pane,
making me jump thirty-five feet into the air.

"Pssst! Clara!" came a voice. I recognized
it straight away, but I still doubted what I was
hearing ... partly because I couldn't actually see
him in the growing darkness, and partly because
it was completely unlike Bradley to be sneaking
around at twilight throwing rocks at a window.

"Bradley?" I pushed my forehead against the
screen.

"Shhhh," he whispered. "Come down, okay?"

I tiptoed past my parents' room, where they
were reading, down the creaky stairs, and out
into the backyard.

"Down here," he whispered when he heard the screen door slide open.

I found him sitting on the bottom tier of my dad's nearly finished deck, half-concealed by a planter box. He was wearing a hoodie, pulled up to conceal most of his face. "What are you doing out here past bedtime?" I asked.

"I'm grounded," he said. "Probably for life ... and that's just the beginning ... but I needed to find out if the cats were okay. Are they? Okay?" There was a tremor in his voice.

"Yeah. They're fine," I whispered. "They're in Shane's garage." But then I couldn't help it. I remembered those posters, and I felt my anger bubble up again. "But don't even think about taking them," I added. Bradley bent his head down so that his face disappeared even more completely into his hoodie. It wasn't until I heard him sniffling that I realized he was probably crying.

"Are you okay?" I asked, but the words came out less gently than they could have.

"Yeah," he answered. I could tell he was lying.

"What happened, anyway?" I asked.

"The construction workers wouldn't let me go until I let them call my parents. When Svetlana found out where I was, she freaked out completely. And then my mom freaked out ten times more when she got home."

I could imagine it. Bradley's mom was a champion freaker-outer. This one time at a sleepover, when she'd caught us sliding down the stairs in our sleeping bags, first she'd yelled, then she'd given us a half-hour lecture about spinal cord injuries, and then she'd threatened to make us sleep without sleeping bags if we did it again ... and that hadn't even been close to as bad as this was.

"In case you were wondering, I didn't tell on you," Bradley went on, sounding kind of annoyed. "I said I was there alone, looking for treasure. And even though the workers told Svetlana that another boy and girl were there, I kept saying I didn't know who they were. Now my mom's taken my metal detector away—probably forever. But at least you and Shane don't have to worry. Plus, she doesn't know about the cats, since I know that's the only thing you care about anyway."

"That's not true!" I objected.

"Okay ... well, the cats and your movie," he added. "And Shane Biggs, who's basically your new best friend."

I glared at him, but Bradley wouldn't even make eye contact.

"He is not my new best friend," I said seriously. I did have to admit that Shane wasn't as bad as I used to think he was. In fact, his unexpected move with the packing tape and weeds had verged on heroic. And, quite possibly for the first time in his life, he seemed to have started to care about someone (or some-cat) other than himself. All afternoon long, he'd been talking to Twinkle Nose in a little baby voice and feeding her bits of bacon. He definitely wasn't my most least favorite person anymore, but he was still on the list.

I didn't say any of that out loud though, because I didn't think I owed Bradley an explanation—not after what he'd done. "Anyway ... all you care about is treasure hunting and your new best friend, Nelson."

"That's not true," Bradley answered.

"Okay, then ... and cat-napping the kittens so you can give them away to your new friends and even to total strangers!"

"I wasn't cat-napping them!" Bradley protested so loudly that we both looked up to make sure my parents hadn't overheard and come to the window. "And I was going to talk to you first before giving any away," he went on in a much softer voice. "I had a five-step interview process planned and everything, to make sure they all went to really good homes. The only reason I was putting the kittens in the box when you found me was because of the bulldozers." He sighed. Then he dug some dirt out from under his fingernails and flicked it away.

"So what were you doing there, then?" I countered. After all, I'd told him to stay away.

"Svetlana was driving me to Nelson's house this morning and I saw that a raccoon had eaten all the food you'd hidden behind the mailbox. I figured the mother cat would be starving, so once I got home, I snuck out to feed her."

Suddenly, I remembered the big bag of cat food, as well as the kitten food and can opener I'd nearly tripped over in the churchyard, and I knew Bradley was telling the truth.

"But you were all out of money," I said.

"Yeah." Bradley shrugged. "I kept hoping I'd find some buried treasure I could sell, but the best thing I've found lately is an old toy car with all the wheels missing. That's why I traded Nelson my dolphin ring for an extra bag of cat food and a tin of kitten food he had in his pantry."

My eyes went wide. The dolphin ring with the real diamond-chip eye? The best treasure Bradley had ever found? The one that was probably worth a hundred dollars?

Bradley sniffed again. "But I guess it was for nothing. I left the food at the churchyard. And we can't go back and get it now, so another raccoon'll probably just eat it."

"Shane and I fed Izzy some bacon," I said. "She's not hungry. And I borrowed some kitten food from Andy's store."

He ran one finger over the wood of the deck. "Well, that's good, I guess," he said. "Anyway ... you don't need to worry about me giving away Izzy-B and the kittens anymore. All the kids at camp who said they'd take one asked their parents, and they all said no, including Nelson's. And not even one person answered my poster yet. Anyway, I should have talked to you before putting them up. I just wanted them to have good homes. But it's like in treasure hunting: finders keepers. You were the one to discover Izzy-B first, so they're your cats."

"Oh," I said, and for a while, I didn't know what else to add. Because of all the things Bradley had just said, here's what got to me the most: For the first time ever, Bradley had called the mother cat Izzy-B instead of Spike. And I guess I should have been happy about that, but something felt all wrong.

"Actually ..." I said, looking up at a star. I focused on its brightness to keep from crying. If Bradley could sacrifice so much—his freedom, his metal detector, and even his dolphin ring with the real diamond-chip eye—for the cat family, then I guessed I could make a sacrifice too, even if it was going to be the most heartbreaking thing I'd ever had to do.

"Her name's not Izzy-B," I said softly. I took a deep breath. "It's Muffy ... and even though I found her, she doesn't belong to me."

@Cat once experienced heartbreak when she realized that, try as she might, she'd never ever catch her own tail.

Adopt-a-Cat-a-Thon

"Kittens! Adorable, cuddly kittens! Adopt one today!"

I've had some dismal days in my life—the day I single-handedly ruined the school track meet by de-wigging the principal, the time I watched Momo's moving van pull out of the driveway, and the time I sabotaged my best friend to try to win a zany game show all come to mind—but the day I had to say goodbye to the kittens was, unexpectedly, not one of them.

"Kittens!" I called out to some passersby. "Come meet the most adorable furry felines in Gleason!"

It was nearing noon on the last Saturday of summer vacation. And finally, after three weeks, our parents (mine, Bradley's, and Shane's) had ended our groundings.

While we'd each been stuck inside our houses with limited TV and computer privileges, Bradley,

Shane, and I had been spending our considerable amounts of free time organizing a grand-scale, community-wide, adopt-a-cat-a-thon fundraiser. And it had all started when my dad had handed me his cell phone.

"We are not keeping any cats," my mom had said in no uncertain terms, after I'd confessed to everything over breakfast.

"Make the call now," Dad added.

So I had dialed, hoping that nobody would be home or—better yet—that the number on the lost-cat poster would be disconnected ... but a woman answered on the first ring.

"Hello. Nancy Goodfellow speaking."

"Um. Hi," I said, feeling very small. "My name's Clara. And I, uh … think I found your cat, Muffy."

First, the woman didn't believe it was really her cat. But after I described Izzy-B in detail, her voice got all choked up. She told me how the cat had gotten out during the big ice storm in late February ... how she'd searched high and low and worried day and night ... how she'd thought she'd never see her again. And, finally, how she'd gotten so lonely that she'd adopted a new cat from the

Humane Society just a few weeks ago.

At first I didn't recognize the woman's voice, but when she said she lived on Peter Street just across from the old church, I put two and two together. "Are you Nancy-Nancy?" I said. "Who knows how to make snapdragons talk?" And it turned out that she was! Izzy-B's owner was the same kind old lady who'd come to my rescue when I'd pretended to fall on the pavement that day.

"What an amazing coincidence!" she marveled. And when we were done saying how strange it was, she asked the question I'd been dreading. "When could I come and get my Muffy?"

"Well," I said. "There's one small problem. Or actually, six ..."

Nancy had come over straightaway, and everyone gathered to meet her: Bradley, Shane, and all our parents. The moment Nancy walked into Shane's garage, Muffy trotted over and rubbed her face against her nylon-covered legs. At first, I thought the cat was having a seizure. "She's shaking!" I pointed at her sides.

But Nancy laughed. "She's purring," she said, bending over stiffly to give Muffy a good ear scratch.

"Oh," I said, feeling silly. I'd seen the mother cat hiss and snarl, growl and meow, but I'd never heard her purr before. I crouched down and held out my hand hopefully, and Izzy-B—I mean, Muffy—came and rubbed against it. She meowed, and then looked up at me with big, round eyes, almost as if to say "Thank you."

"Well, look at that," Nancy said. "I've had a lot of cats in my life, but Muffy isn't like the rest. How can I put it nicely?" Nancy looked off to one side. "She's persnickety," she decided. "She doesn't tend to get along with people other than me."

I felt my cheeks flush with pride. Then Nancy clapped a hand over her mouth. "Oh my goodness. There they are!" At the sight of Twinkle Nose, Prickle, and Pickle coming out of their cardboard box, Nancy's eyes welled up with tears—and she hadn't even seen Peary, Rosie, and Bouncer yet, who were the cutest ones, if you asked me.

I had to admit: I hadn't thought it was possible for the kittens to get more adorable, but—as Shane put it—they leveled up with each passing day. At four weeks and two days, their cuteness had definitely peaked, though. If they got any sweeter,

AHHHH!
TOO CUTE!

people who saw them might literally explode.

Even Bradley's mom—who did not like cats—had crouched down on the garage floor to scratch Prickle's ears. And my dad was smiling as Twinkle Nose batted at his shoelace.

"You know, I'd take them all if I could," Nancy said sadly. She reached down to let Pickle sniff her fingers.

"I know," I said. We'd already talked about this on the phone when I'd told Nancy Muffy's big news. Nancy felt that the kittens were her responsibility. After all, she'd let her cat escape from her house when she was just seven months old—before she had been spayed. I told her not to feel bad (after all, I knew how cunning Izzy-B could be—it was part of why I loved her), but Nancy still felt rotten about what had happened.

All the same, she couldn't look after seven cats at

her age (eight, if you counted the new cat she'd just adopted). And since kittens were supposed to stay with their mother until they were fully weaned, Muffy couldn't go home with her yet either. Luckily, Janet saved the day by offering up her garage to the cat family for the rest of the month, with a few conditions.

"The kids will need to find homes for all the kittens," she'd suggested as we stood there watching them play. "And take care of them until they're ready to leave their mother."

"And that doesn't just mean playing with them," my mom added when she'd caught me, Bradley, and Shane grinning at each other. "It also means cleaning the litter box at least twice a day."

Then, when my dad had pointed out that I absolutely needed to pay Andy back every cent for the cat food I'd borrowed and lost, and replace his deck-building supplies, the seed of an idea had come to me. And once I'd shared it with Bradley and Shane, it had grown, and grown, and grown until there we were, hosting an event so large it spanned three front yards.

In my yard, I was selling a bunch of my stuff to

make the money I'd need to pay my debts. But I'd also gotten the whole street involved. The week before, I'd gone door to door asking for donations of used stuff to sell to raise money for a cause that was very close to my heart.

Meanwhile, my dad had set up the GrillMaster Legend in our driveway so he could sell hamburgers—not to mention show off his new toy to the neighbors. (He'd also been giving deck tours to anyone he could convince to come into the backyard.)

Next door, in Shane's yard, the adoption tent was set up. And Mrs. Patrinas had agreed to let us use her yard for face painting and a silent auction, as long as no one trampled her petunias.

I watched as a grinning kid ran past holding a bright-red sno-cone in her hands—made by the machine I'd given Bradley for his birthday. Based on the cat whiskers on her cheeks, I could tell she was another satisfied customer who had hopefully dropped a few coins into the donation box after my mom had finished painting her face.

"Guess what?" Shane was bounding toward me. He had a huge smile on his face. It almost made him hard to recognize. "My mom says I can adopt a kitten. Isn't that great?"

"What?!" I said indignantly, and then I turned and pretended to be rearranging some mystery novels on a table so he wouldn't see that I was about to cry. It was SO unfair! Even Bradley's mom—who'd been angrier than the rest of our parents combined—had been impressed by how responsible he'd been with the kittens the last few weeks. She'd decided to let Bradley get a pet just a few days before. It was only a fish, but still!

"I picked Twinkle Nose," Shane went on, "only I'm changing her name to Dragor."

Dragor? I hadn't thought there was a worse name than Spike for a cat, but apparently there was. "You can come play with her sometimes," he offered kindly, and I felt my outrage soften just a little. Because the truth was, the kittens needed forever families, and Shane and Janet had a warm and happy home. Living there was going to be good for Twinkle Nose—I mean, Dragor. And having a pet to love (and hopefully to distract him from playing video games all day) was also going to be good for Shane. The cat family had already changed him in some ways I hadn't thought possible.

"That's great, Shane," I said, giving him a small smile. And I mostly actually meant it.

Then thankfully (before I had to act completely happy for him any longer) my dad came toward us with two reusable plates. "Who wants hamburgers and veggie burgers?" he asked, holding them out. I grabbed one.

"Wait, Clara! That's not the veggie burger!" he said. But before he could take it back, I shoved it into my mouth and took a big, satisfying bite.

"Ohmygosh, isso good," I mumbled.

My dad shrugged and offered the veggie one to Shane, but he shook his head, so Dad took a bite of it instead. "Wow." He made a face. I nodded. I recognized them as the Value Brand veggie burgers we'd bought before, and I knew all too well what he was tasting. "So ... does this mean you're not a vegetarian anymore?" Dad asked, after he'd managed to swallow.

My mouth was full, but I tipped my hand from side to side in answer. Since the day Shane and I had fed bacon to Izzy-B, I'd had a craving for meat

I couldn't control. And what's more, now that it had become clear that our internet cat movie was not going to make millions of dollars, I'd come to realize that my dream of saving *all* animals was probably a touch unrealistic—at least for the time being. But just because I couldn't save them all didn't mean I couldn't save some.

A flyer had recently come in the mail about a vegetarian cooking class at the

Wait! @Cat! The fish don't need saving!

EASY!

GASP!

The time the zoo boat sank and @Cat saved ALL the animals.

community center. I was planning to convince my dad to enroll with me to learn some good meat-free recipes. I even had a schedule in mind for my family: Meatless Mondays, Every-Second-Tuesday Tofu Nights, and Animal-Friendly Fridays.

Also, while planning the adopt-a-thon, I'd discovered that there were already organizations right in my own city that were working hard to help animals. At least until I was old enough to dedicate my life to the cause (which I was totally planning to do), I could make a difference by helping them.

"Look!" I pointed down the sidewalk. A car with a logo of a cat and a dog on the side had just pulled up. "The lady from the Humane Society is here. Should we get things started?"

Shane nodded, so I flagged down Bradley (who'd been manning the adoption table) and motioned for him to join us at the microphone.

"Ahem." I cleared my throat. "Everyone. If I could have your attention, please."

The neighbors, strangers, and little kids who'd been milling around the three yards started to gather around Shane's porch, where the microphone and speakers my dad had borrowed from the hardware store were set up.

"We'd like to thank you all for coming to our Cat Adopt-a-Thon and Charity Fundraiser for the Gleason Humane Society." I handed the mic to Shane, who had prepared a little speech to introduce our guest—a woman named Morgan who ran the cat adoption program at the Humane Society. She had long blonde hair that hung in a thick braid down her back. Her cat-and-mouse earrings danced when she took the microphone from Shane and started talking, waving her hands excitedly.

First, she said how important it is to spay or neuter your cat—which wasn't all that interesting (I mean, I already knew that), but then she moved on to a much more riveting subject: us!

"We're so thankful for citizens like Clara, Bradley, and Shane—people who, when they find stray cats or kittens, take care of them and help them to find forever families," she said. "Which is what today's all about."

As she went on, I looked out over the crowd. There were at least forty people there—including Andy from the Milk 'n' Variety, Nancy, all the neighbors on the street, and even some of Bradley's camp friends ... including Nelson—who was starting to grow on me.

He'd returned Bradley's dolphin ring with the real diamond-chip eye (which

BLING!

Bradley had decided to donate to the silent auction). Plus, Nelson had brought along one of his own metal-detector finds to auction off: an old coin that he swore was worth a ton of money because the eagle on it was looking in the wrong direction. I doubted anyone was going to pay more than twenty-five cents for it, but it was the thought that counted.

All in all, it was a good turnout—and so far, several people had adopted kittens. I could tell from the smiles on the adoptive families' faces that Bouncer, Prickle, and Pickle were going to good homes … but the happiest and saddest part for me came when Peary found his home—and it wasn't with me.

"He's gonna make a real good shop cat," Andy had said, letting my favorite kitten nuzzle his finger through the bars of the cat carrier. "Keep the mice out of the storage room for me. And keep me company while he's at it. And you'll come visit him often," the shopkeeper added when he'd seen the tears in my eyes.

I scratched the kitten's chin in the spot he liked best and promised that I would. If he couldn't be with me, I honestly couldn't think of a better home for Peary than the Milk 'n' Variety.

Morgan finished her speech just then and handed the mic to Bradley. We'd planned everything down to the second, so I knew he was going to talk about the kind of care cats and kittens needed, and then I was going to bring it all home with a heartfelt plea to adopt a kitten today and donate to the Humane Society ... only Bradley veered way off script.

"We're going to talk about adopting kittens in a few minutes," he said, "but first we have a special presentation to make." I watched in confusion as Janet opened the front door and came out with a collapsible screen. Meanwhile, my dad was busy rolling some kind of projector onto Shane's lawn.

"The internet is full of cat videos," Bradley said while they worked, "but the film you're about to see takes cat cinema to a new level. *@Cat and the Unstoppable 6* is easily the most action-packed feline-focused internet film of the year. And it was directed by our very own Clara Humble." He held out one arm toward me and the crowd clapped politely.

I was stunned. So stunned that Bradley had to drag me out of the way of the screen when the film started.

As the intro music began and @Cat flew across the screen for the first time, the whole crowd seemed entranced. In fact, Bradley and I were the only ones who weren't watching ... but that was only because I'd seen it at least a hundred times, and Bradley seemed to have something he wanted to say.

Over the weeks that we'd been planning the adopt-a-thon, we'd talked, of course, but it was all business. We hadn't really made up after our big fight, and whenever we'd been alone with the kittens together, things had been weird.

"Clara ..." he started, looking down at his feet. "I didn't mean it when I said your movie was a bad idea." He glanced up at the screen. "It's actually incredible. Especially the part at the end where Poodle Noodle explodes in a million pieces with that cool fireball effect in the background."

"Shhhh!" A little boy who was standing near us glared at Bradley. "Spoilers!"

Bradley made an "oops" face. "Anyway," Bradley

went on, more quietly. "Even if it doesn't make you internet-famous"—he squeezed his lips together, and then kind of mumbled the next part—"you'll always be famous to me."

By then, the film had reached its most heart-wrenching scene—the one where @Cat discovers the Unstoppable 6 alone on a street corner and vows to be their loyal friend and protector till the end. And as the tear-jerking music swelled, I threw my arms around Bradley and hugged him hard.

"And you'll always be a famous treasure hunter to me." I let him go and then added, "Even if you only find tin cans."

And I knew something else was true too: It was always going to be me and Bradley against the world.

GLEASON TIMES

GRAND OPENING OF THE AMAZING ANTIQUE ALUMINUM-CAN MUSEUM!

MUSEUM

CAN YOU DIG IT?
THE CAN MAN CAN!

If Bradley ever starts a tin-can museum, I'll be first in line at the grand opening.

Or, at least, I wanted it to be. "Friends again?" I asked tentatively.

"Well, duh!" Bradley smiled, and then he hesitated a second. "But I'm still going to be friends with Nelson too, okay?"

I looked over into the crowd to where Nelson was standing. He was nodding his head thoughtfully at the part where @Cat has to make a tough moral decision: Is it kinder to let kittens be kittens, or nobler to train them to fight crime? Despite being way too serious, he was basically a decent person. I could probably grow to like him. I mean, if I had to spend time with him.

"And I'm still going to go treasure hunting and metal detecting—and you can do stuff with animals and make movies," Bradley went on. "I mean, just because we're best friends doesn't mean we need to like the same stuff or spend all our time together, right?"

I grimaced a little at that. We were growing up. I guess it was only natural that we wanted to do and try different things—but it still hurt a little to think that we wouldn't always be doing them together like we used to. I sighed. If being ten was this complicated, I could only imagine what the higher ages were going to be like.

"Wait!" I said suddenly, giving my head a little shake. "I just got it!"

Bradley looked confused. "Got what?"

"The riddle!" I said. "Sorry. I'll be right back!"

I pushed my way through the crowd, accidentally almost spilling a kid's cup of lemonade all over her, and then I totally interrupted the conversation Andy was having with Mrs. Patrinas—but this couldn't wait another second.

"Your age!" I announced breathlessly. "It's your age!" I repeated, when Andy looked baffled. "What goes up but never comes down. Your age, right?"

"Oh, don't I know it." Mrs. Patrinas laughed, stretching out a kink in her back.

Andy nodded. "By gum, she got it again!" he said proudly. He reached down and gave Peary a scratch through the bars of his carrier. "Watch out for this one, Peary," he said to his kitten. "She's getting smarter every day."

Suddenly, I felt so much better. That riddle had been driving me crazy for weeks!

"Thanks, Andy," I called, and then I ran back

through the crowd.

There was something else that had been driving me crazy too, and I needed to get it off my chest. "About the chicken game ... from your party ..." I said when I reached Bradley again.

"Can we play it tomorrow?" he asked before I could even finish my question.

"Really?" I'd been about to ask if he'd thought it was dumb and babyish. I'd never felt more relieved in my life.

"Yeah," Bradley answered. "I thought of a really good one. I'm keeping it a surprise, but it involves the chicken, a tennis racket, and a spray can of whipped cream." He started giggling. I could hardly wait to see it—whatever it was.

"Oh, but can we do it in the afternoon?" he added kind of sheepishly. He was looking toward Mrs. Patrinas' yard, where a few of his camp friends were gathered, geeking out over Nelson's rare quarter. "I have some plans in the morning."

I felt jealous of Bradley's new friends, but only for a second. "Okay," I said. The fact was, I'd never be able to make myself care all that much about old coins, rust-covered buttons, and dented jewelry ...

and that was okay.

Just because I didn't love treasure hunting didn't mean I couldn't love that Bradley loved it. Or that he couldn't love that I loved caring for animals and aspiring to cinematic excellence.

We might be growing up, but that didn't have to mean growing apart ... not as long as we didn't want it to.

"If you're not too busy after we play the chicken game," I said, "I might have a project we can work on together. It has something for both of us." I took a folded piece of paper out of my pocket and showed him.

Spike the Fish and Bijou the Brave in ...
THE MYTHICAL LOST JEWELS OF THE DEEP
In a world where chinchillas and fish so seldom cross paths ...

... two unlikely friends form a bond that cannot be denied, and discover a treasure that has been lost for centuries ...

PRODUCED BY: Clara Humble and Bradley Degen
FILMED BY: Shane Biggs

"Nice!" Bradley smiled. "I like it. Only ..." He grimaced. "Wait a sec." He grabbed a pencil from the adoption table and made a few adjustments.

Spike the Mini-Shark   @Cat
~~Spike the fish~~ and ~~Bijou the Brave~~ in ...
THE MYTHICAL LOST JEWELS OF THE DEEP

"I dunno," I said. "I like the shark part, but Bijou's not really cut out to play @Cat. She'll try to eat the antenna."

Bradley grinned over my shoulder and I turned to see Nancy walking toward me with a cat carrier. My parents were behind her. She handed the cage to me with tears in her eyes.

"My new cat, Muffy Two, she's on the persnickety side as well," Nancy said in a shaky voice. "As much as I miss Muffy, I can't see it working out between them. Your parents tell me you've always wanted a cat of your own, and that you just had a big birthday."

I looked to my mom and dad for confirmation, and they both nodded. I couldn't lie: I'd tried to act thrilled when, the week before, they'd given me a little video camera for my tenth birthday, but it hadn't been easy. Obviously, I'd really been hoping they'd change their minds about a kitten—but this?! Somehow, this was even better.

I set the cage down on the grass and put my fingers in between the bars just as the movie music swelled and the big climactic finish neared.

"Did you hear that, Muffy?" I said. "I get to take you home!" The mother cat didn't nuzzle me lovingly, but she didn't hiss either.

"Wait here!" Bradley said. "I'll go get Spike. I want to introduce them right away." He took off across the lawn so he could cut through my backyard to get his fish bowl.

"Clara!" Shane called out from his porch. The movie credits were rolling. "Come take a bow."

I handed Izzy-B's carrier to my dad and ran up the steps so I could bask in the crowd's applause. (I mean, I had kind of earned it.) But first, I grabbed Shane's arm and made him bow with me, because he'd earned it too.

After the second round of applause, I made one last plea to the crowd to adopt a kitten, and then I waved them away humbly. People began to disperse, making their way over to the garage sale, the adoption table, and the silent auction, and I ran back to get Muffy.

As the adopt-a-thon went on around us, I sat down on the grass beside her carrier and took out my storyboard to make a few more changes. And as I worked, I smiled to myself. I couldn't help it. Even though @*Cat and the Unstoppable 6* had finished its first public screening mere seconds ago, I was already looking forward to what was next. I just had a feeling it was going to be a brand-new, better-than-ever sequel to a very old friendship.

THE END

WHAT'S BETTER THAN ONE CLARA HUMBLE BOOK?

THREE Clara Humble books!

Follow Clara as she goes from sassy (semi) superhero to gutsy game-show gal to courageous kitty crusader!